The Awakening

By Frank Talaber

Photo By SueB Photography

Print ISBN: 978-1-7770978-5-6

Cover art by
Miblart

Stillwaters Runs Deep Book Three: The Awakening

How angry would a mythical god be if he found himself awakening inside a mortal? After a strange and inexplicable death inside a jail, an intriguing and extraordinary shaman detects great unrest in the world, and breaks his way into the jail to investigate. He enlists Detective Carol Ainsworth to assist as an undercover prison officer who, rather strangely, also finds herself tasked with bringing to justice the murderer of a gentle forest being's mother.

Prelude

Water lapping at his feet, Charlie awoke alone on the beach, cold, shuddering and naked. Mist rolled in waves, clinging to everything with its clammy, smothering embrace.

He caught shadows shifting. The mist circled around a figure emerging from the sodden grip of trees lining the shore. Thunder shook overhead and lightning danced like snakes frying.

He closed his eyes and it began again.

* * *

An eye opens after eons of sleep. It breathes deep. *At last. I smell him.*

Table of contents

Dedication 5
Prelude 7
Chapter One 11
Chapter Two 31
Chapter Three 51
Chapter Four 67
Chapter Five 85
Chapter Six 101
Chapter Seven 111
Chapter Eight 127
Chapter Nine 141
Chapter Ten 159
Chapter Eleven 179
Chapter Twelve 193
Chapter Thirteen 201
Chapter Fourteen 207
Chapter Fifteen 213
Chapter Sixteen 217
Chapter Seventeen 221
Chapter Eighteen 229
Chapter Nineteen 241
Epilogue 247
About the Author 254
The Ainsworth Chronicles 259

Chapter One

"What makes you think you qualify for this job?" asked the stern-looking white man heading the hiring committee.

"Well, I'm native aren't I?" Charlie responded, smiling at him and the six other Caucasian members of the review board. He figured they felt protected behind their heavy desks, wanting him to feel exposed in the one chair centred in the large stark, empty office. He tapped his cane on the floor. "Nice."

One raised a head and stared at him.

"Real wood, pine, probably eighty years old. Nice stuff." He smiled back.

The five-man, two-woman board flipped through the pages on their clipboards desperately hoping to find other applications. There weren't any, and his didn't take much reading.

"And being a man of deep spiritual connections, I reckoned this was up my alley. If you look under 'Hobbies' you'll see I love to watch baseball."

"Yes," the same man said dryly. "Montreal Expos in particular. I do believe they no longer exist."

"Yeah, go those Blue Jays." Charlie beamed at the man. "Been meaning to get a new cap, rather attached to this old friend though, we've been through a lot. Although I guess for special occasions like this I should've splurged, look a little more respectable. If I get a spending budget on this job, could afford a new cap."

"Ah, yes." The man reading the resume cleared his throat. The scowl on his face showed he wasn't much of a baseball fan or any kind of sports fan for that matter. "You also cite 'watching documentaries' as well as baseball. These aren't really hobbies, Mr. ah, Stillwater."

"Charlie."

"What?"

"It's not Ah Stillwater. It's Charlie Stillwater-S." He smiled and leaned on his cane. "I guess you could be right. Watching the Expos was more like my passion. Got hooked on them after they were top of the standings in eighty-four and probably would have taken the World Series if it wasn't for the strike. Eighty-four. Man, that's been awhile. I guess it is time for a new cap, or at least get this one cleaned. As for the documentaries, I think Dr. Suzuki has for the most part got it right. Bit slow to figure things out, but the man's on the right path. I think he's Chinese. Oops, I mean Oriental. Don't want to be politically incorrect these days. But I reckon he's got some native blood in him. I like the guy, looks a lot like my uncle Ralph."

The committee flipped through their blank pages again, wishing at least one other application would materialize. They were disappointed.

"It's hard finding anyone willing to relocate to Prince Rupert to fill any position, but especially in the psychological fields," one rather well-nourished woman whispered to the cookie-cutter figure next to her. "I remind you that the head warden has warned that if a candidate isn't found by the end of this week, one of us will have to go in and deal with them and I for one am not walking in there with the vile creatures. The way their dirty eyes linger, undressing me." She shivered and flushed a deep red, either embarrassed or aroused by the thought. "I wouldn't be caught alone with any of them in a cell, probably get raped. I'll quit if we don't get someone."

The head interviewer looked at his papers again and back at the others. "I agree. The natives are starting to get out of hand. We'll take on Mr. Shaman man, let him try to deal with them. Better he gets assaulted than one of us. We have our Elder, the jail keeps its licence and after the Federal inspector leaves next week, we either fire him or find another to fill in. I request we send out a new listing for the position." The suits all nodded their agreement.

He cleared his throat. "Okay, Mr. Ah, Charlie Stillwater, we'll give you a two week trial."

"Oh good. Ends on a night of the full moon." Charlie smiled. "I'll be feeling a mite hairy then. Should bring my silver razor for protection."

They glared at him. "Won't last a day," one stern woman whispered to the colleague next to her. "Arrogant bastard, but feed him to the wolves instead of one of us. I agree."

"I'll be surprised if he lasts two hours. But we have no choice. It's him or one of us. We file the paperwork, get our federal funding. If he quits, well, we'll have to hope we get a better response next time. Everyone agreed?" he whispered to the others. They nodded back.

"Ahem! Be reminded Mr. Charlie Stillwater, that you've few credentials. No psychiatric training of any kind, not even tribal endorsements to prove that you are the shaman you claim to be. However, if you are a shaman, even self-taught, it does help you qualify for the position of Native Elder that we are seeking. You'll really need to prove yourself though. This is no place for amateurs. We're dealing with dangerous persons in here, killers, sociopaths, psychopaths and rapists."

"Well, I didn't think this would be a kindergarten picnic. These folks aren't here just because they tripped up grandma at the bus stop. I've got me trusty bag and this…", he tapped the side of his head with his orca headed cane. “A full deck of marbles, that don’t rattle. Oh, I didn’t mention that I’ve watched the original Karate Kid eighteen times, got the crane kick down pat. Try me.”

The overweight woman choked down her disgust. “I think some discussion should be made regarding certain standards of uniform ethics later. However you’re the best candidate so far. So, before we change our minds, we are offering you the position. Sign this agreement so we can pass our findings to the warden.” He shoved a paper towards him. Charlie leaned forward and scrawled his John Hancock.

“Well, you can count on me to get the job done. I’ve always had my trusty cane and my wits. Never failed me yet. Although come to think of it I’m pretty good at outside animal management. Should have put that on my resume.”

“Outside... Animal ...Management...” one of the team slowly muttered aloud, like he couldn’t believe what his ears had just received.

“I’ve handled some irate squirrels in my backyard. They’ll never figure out where I’ve hidden those nuts. And a rather troublesome raccoon I named Rocky, although he tells me he likes Raymond better, raccoons are like that you know. Dealt with a pesky Raven too and he was more difficult to deal with than you could imagine but that’s a whole ‘nother story. Everything I needed to know I learned from my elders and from out there in the wilderness. Does this job include lunch and my own office?” He looked about tapping his cane on the floor.

“There is a canteen here. Meals are included.”

“Well, this could be an interesting two weeks and at least I’ll get some free grub. Should have brought my other jacket, it’s got bigger pocket for leftovers. Oh, and no name plaque.”

“Name plaque?”

"Yeah, on the door to my office. I don't care for titles. Besides after a few days I think I should remember which office was mine."

"If you last that long Mr. Stillwater."

He retreated to the back of the room and reached for the doorknob. "And we'll talk about a raise in two weeks. This should be my kind of job, dealing with natives, riffraff and awful canteen food. Man, I should have applied for this earlier." He laughed. "Don't reckon the food will be up to the organic stuff I usually eat when I'm out in the woods, but hey, its food. And free. Now that's a bonus plan." He tilted his button-festooned Expos cap. "So I'm off to check on the rabble. How long before I begin to build towards a pension?"

The main interviewer, now almost regretting his decision, closed his eyes. "You've a client to deal with later this afternoon. The pension you'll be building towards from your first paycheque. Now get to work, Mr. Stillwater. We'll file the contract with the warden this afternoon. All the details regarding benefits, pay and holidays will be in it."

"Yes boss. And you can call me Charlie. Boss. Hmm. Never had a boss before, this could be fun. Holidays! You mean I can get time off and fly to exotic locations, like LA? Never been to Leduc, Alberta. Some distant cousins out there." He turned and wandered off into the corridor.

"One hour! I give him one hour."

"Yeah, but at least none of us have to go in there to deal with THEM." The overweight woman grunted. "And I for one, hope he gets what he deserves."

* * *

Charlie limped down the hall, leaning on his orca-headed cane, whistling. "Oh, I forgot to tell them I don't do suits and ties. Although a new plaid shirt would be nice, I think I got this one in ninety-three."

He winked at one of the guards as he led a prisoner down the hall. "Great day, lovely day. Nice uniform."

The guard scowled back as the prisoner glared at Charlie. "Oh, I must admit that pin stripe does make you look rather thin." He said to the guard as they passed.

"Who the fuck is that?" the prisoner grumbled.

"Don't know and none of your damn business anyways. Get a move on." He pushed him forward.

"Charlie Stillwaters, your new Native Elder." He whistled, again tapping the walls and floor with his cane. "Could use a bit of more cheery paint colour. Will have to suggest that to the warden. Okay, time for some lunch and then off to work. Off to work, man can't say I've ever said that before."

* * *

In the darkness I wait.
Humming songs, like I always did, ever since it could remember.
Waiting.
Knowing they would come.

I smile and hum another song.
Waiting.

* * *

Charlie grabbed his meal tray and sat down at the only empty table in the canteen. The inmates stared and snickered to each other. "Must be the hat. Obviously jealous," he muttered as he began to dig into his soup.

A large shadow blocked out the glow of florescent. "You're at my table," barked a heavy gruff voice.

Charlie looked up and gulped. A virtual mountain of a man stood before him. Native, with greasy dark hair, deep set eyes, face contorted into a nasty grimace. Standing well over six foot, bordering on seven, and nearly four hundred pounds. Not much of which was fat, but mostly anger buried in several large chips on his shoulder. The tables held at least six, nearly every table full, except for the one that only Charlie sat at. "There's plenty of room for two of us."

The babble of conversation ceased, spoons hung in the air. A dollop of soup echoed with a plop as everyone stopped to watch the unfolding massacre. This, Charlie knew could go well or totally sideways, like a hockey player getting slammed into the boards head down, not looking.

"You . . . are . . . sitting . . . at . . . my . . . fucking . . . table," growled the mass that made Rocky Mountains look small. Great meaty fists grated on the lunch tray.

Charlie didn't really think getting thumped on his first day would make a good impression on the others. "You've a licence for that hotdog stand?" Charlie waved his hand.

"What?"

A single fly buzzing reverberated through the canteen. Several breaths inhaled.

"A hotdog stand."

The behemoth stood gritting his teeth. "What the hell you going on about?" Charlie could tell the giant's puzzlement was winning over the rage to crush the annoying insect before him. Which he could in one swat, like a grizzly tagging a poodle. "Your fly is undone."

The man lifted his tray, looked down and blushed.

A sneer cracked one side of his mouth, intimidation at its best, backed by three hundred plus pounds of muscle. He looked at Charlie and laughed. "Move the fuck over. For an old bastard, you're alright."

He thumped the tray down, slopping some of the soup, and sat next to the suddenly relieved shaman who'd just seen his next three lifetimes sail before his eyes. After zipping his fly, he thumped Charlie on the back. Charlie gagged, nearly swallowing his back and front teeth at the same time. "Hey, you're okay. Most people are usually scared of me."

The other inmates blinked in disbelief, looking from each other to the no longer impeding demise of the newest member of staff, thinking they'd just seen the Titanic miss the iceberg and land at New York, before returning disappointedly to their meals.

"Well of course they would be. Yours are the size of a pair of grizzly bears stacked on top of each other in a totem, wearing the grimace of the bottom one suffering from fighting off the butt of the other after he ate a load of Tacos." Charlie stuck out his tongue and squinted his eyes like he'd just smelled fresh cow patty.

The big man laughed again. Puzzlement showed on the other inmates' faces, not understanding what was going on and rather disappointed that today's massacre had turned into a Laurel and Hardy love-in. Most had never even seen him smile let alone heard him laugh out loud, nor say more than three words in any one sitting. "Who are you?"

Charlie knew humour was rare on this one's face by the well-ingrained frown lines. "Charlie Stillwaters. Your new Prison Elder." He stuck his hand forward after wiping it on his jean jacket.

"I'm Thomas Johnson." He shook the shaman's hand, somewhat gently, although Charlie's eyes opened as far as they could as the natural muscle crumpled three of his fingers into his elbow.

"Wow, bet the Man of Steel would have a bitch of a time winning against you in an arm wrestle. Your real name?"

"That is my real name."

"Raised in a residential school?"

"Yeah! How'd you know?"

"It's my job to know," he lied, thinking he should sound like he knew something about being a legal Prison Elder, even though he was only a half day into the job. "No, I meant the real name your parents gave you."

He frowned. "My parents died when I was very young. Don't know my real name, or if I have one."

"Well I'm naming you with your native name. Now then, I'm thinking its T'aalgii Tilldagaaw Xuuajii, Big Mountain Grizzly."

The man ladled soup into his mouth, pausing for thought. "Big Mountain. I like that." Charlie breathed deeply, realizing he'd just befriended undoubtedly the best, or perhaps worst, guy in the place. The one everyone else feared.

"Charles Stillwater report to the warden's office." Spoke the disembodied voice over the PA.

"Duty calls." Charlie rose. "Didn't like the soup anyways, too salty. I'll have to talk to the cook about that and give them heck. I told them it's Charlie Stillwater-S. Government never can get things right. Probably have to redo all six hundred and forty pages of the contract. Did know you they only allow me two urine breaks and nine ounces of coffee? A day? Man, might have to buy diapers to make it through."

Big Mountain laughed and wiped the back of his hand across his mouth and slid Charlie's tray towards himself. "I'll eat the rest of your soup then, and you're welcome at my table anytime. But don't any of you other bastards get any ideas," he grumbled loudly to the others. "And if you need someone to back you up in here..." he said more softly, and winked at Charlie.

"Tell you what, if you want I could dig into your files and see if I could find out some background history."

"I'd like that. Told I had a sister, but never met her."

"I'll see what I can do and no cracking any heads while I'm on shift. You wouldn't want to make me mad, I crack a mean face." Charlie cracked several ridiculous faces as he got up. Big Mountain snorted a load of soup out of his nose, gagging.

"Quick! He's choking! Someone get Arnold Schgartabugger to perform mouth to mouth, cause no one else is going to press lips to the Griz here and walk away without missing limbs."

The big man laughed even harder, turning puce. Charlie slapped him on the back several times until the big man spit a chunk of food out.

"Hey, funny place to hide a Colt .45," he said looking up at the approaching guards. They reached for their guns. "Oh just kidding, it's just a chunk of hot dog, shaped like a gun." The two guards looked at him like he was mad. Griz just wiped at the tears of laughter running down his cheeks.

Walking away, Charlie realized he'd just found his first client as an Elder and his first prison friend.

* * *

I am a being, alone, entirely alone. Except there are others. I want to meet the others. I want to be me. Only who am I?

I had others in my life. Older, parents. Then why am I here?

Alone?

And who? The question remains. Of who?

Am I?

* * *

"So this is where the last Elder expired. Don't disturb anything. They're still not sure whether it's a crime or an accident. Wish they'd make their minds up so we don't have to spend shifts guarding a damn tent." The guard indicated his work-mate whose duty today was to babysit the scene so it couldn't be tampered with. "My turn tomorrow." The yellow Police Line Do Not Cross tape surrounding the sweat lodge in the grounds behind the penitentiary sagged and swayed in the breeze.

"Boy, you guys aren't very sociable around here. No wonder you can't get any help. Darn it though," he tut-tutted as he walked around the sweat lodge, "I wanted to arrange a really swanky soiree tonight. You know, tux, champagne and horses douvres."

"It's hors d'oeuvres, I believe," the man grumbled, "and those are big words for a native."

"I watch a lot of educational TV. Gives you a large vocabulary. You know, documentaries, educational programs and the like. Pick up the odd phrase. I bet you like to watch tripe like all of those insipid reality shows."

"Yeah, how'd you know that?"

"Just a wild guess. Rots your mind that stuff." Charlie continued pacing around the sweat lodge trying to get a sense of what may have happened here. This was the reason he'd received some weird calls from the spirits in his dreams recently. Only why, he wasn't sure. A death didn't usually raise such unrest from the spirit world. He knew that no one inside would leave until the sweat was done, although on the usual sessions they often took three breaks to cool down, one for each of the four directions. Once inside, there would be very little light to see by, only the glow of the rocks, which had been burning for hours. The person leading, usually but not always the Elder himself would be moving about, flapping eagles' feathers and other objects for effect, but how a murder could be committed with not one of the inhabitants noticing was a mystery. The guard scowled as he followed the still-pacing Charlie. "Do you have a list of the people in the group?"

"I don't, but the office does, and the police and WCB. Why are you asking? Figure one of your relatives was in on it or you decided to become the next Dick Tracy?" the guard, Jenkins grumbled, obviously put off by having to hang around while Charlie checked out the scene.

"Just curious as to how someone could have died without anyone noticing. I'll have to lead a sweat sooner or later. WCB?"

"All accidents or deaths at work are treated as just 'work related incidents', unless foul play can be determined. If I was you, I'd hope they'd find any killer damn quick before they had to start asking for applications for my replacement." He snickered at what he thought was a great joke.

Charlie sniffed the air ignoring the guard's threats. Death never left a pleasant aroma but a murder created a foul stench. He sniffed again, loudly. Odd, no lingering after tones. Almost as if... he sniffed again.

"Hey, you got allergies, short of coke or something? There's plenty of drugs around this place, no matter how hard we try to police the inmates." His walkie-talkie went off. "Time to go. I've got duties besides babysitting you, old man."

"Some of us can sense and smell things better than most animals. Any chance you were on duty that day?" Charlie inhaled again, overly loudly.

"Yeah. What's it to ya?"

"Oh, just asking." He knew one thing, this guard was not only belligerent, but possibly capable of murder. He'd keep an eye on him. Charlie inhaled again. The wood-smoke of the sweat had covered the subtle floating aromas, but there was something underlying everything here. Something worse than menacing. The spirits were right. There was something very unnatural here.

"The only animal I want to smell is frying cow, as in a burger. Now time to beat it."

"There!" he yelled.

The guard jumped, "What the fuck..."

Charlie stopped and moved his head side to side, sniffing loudly. It was gone. Out of the corner of his eye he caught the shadow of something moving on the edge of the forest, by the fences.

"You, old man, are the freakiest bastard I ever met and I'll tell you I've met quite the collection of freaks here. Now get moving. Sniffing time is over, or go join the hound dog society if that's your bag."

Charlie moved to the doorway, careful not to disturb the tape or scene. He'd have to come back alone. There was something lurking there alright, something masking everything else under the smell of sweat and wood-smoke. Something fouler than death. The spirits usually weren't wrong about getting him here. He glanced past the grounds to the dark edge of the forest.

A branch shifted.

And he'd been watched. *Yup most curious. And since I can't get into the lodge or the adjacent women's prison, I think I need to contact some-*

one who can. Going to need some help on this one and I know just the person that owes me a favour.

* * *

The floor bed shook. From a dark cave one eye opened, then another. It looked around in the darkness before stretching slowly from the cramped form it had endured all this time. Poking its head up into the ocean's waters, the creature took one deep sniff. The salty waters told it all it needed to know.

It is time. We need to act again.

It let out a high pitched squeal to the others, also long buried. The ground shook in response.

But first a feeding. *It has been a very long time since we've awoken and I'm sure the others are, like me, famished.*

And it knew who would do.

* * *

Charlie strode down the hall towards his office. There was something out there watching him, he knew it. As he left the washroom he turned the corner and ran into two men dressed in suits. Charlie glanced at the name tag on the one that said Warden.

"Oh, the big guy, the big Cheese, el capitain, the dude who signs my paycheque."

"Who the hell are you Sir?"

"Charlie Stillwaters"

"Not on any payroll I know of around here."

"We hired him this morning, sir. Remember the 'I need an Elder pronto or we lose our Federal funding for the next six months,' speech?"

"Yes, what was that got to do with this, I might say, disheveled looking, fellow?"

"Your new Elder counsellor, Boss Man." He grabbed the warden's hand and shook it hard three times before wiping his hand on his shirt. "Crap, forgot to dry my hands after that last trip to the pisser. Actually didn't notice any paper dispensers in the cans. But you should have someone look into those vacuum cleaner ducts they've installed in the washroom. Makes lots of noise, but didn't pick much off the floor. Oh and no ties. I don't do ties. Yours I'll have to admit is rather smart. Solid one colour, denotes lack of character, bland in tastes and preferences, but very dapper, as they say in England. Goes well with the fancy cufflinks. Gotta run, don't want the boss to think I'm loitering about on my first day. Need to make a good first impression and all."

With that Charlie sauntered off, limping on his cane. Still wiping his hands as he muttered more to himself than anyone else. "Glad that wasn't a number two."

"Sorry sir, there weren't any other applications."

The warden stood there blinking, calmly pulled a hanky from his vest pocket and wiped his damp hand. "Henricks, in my fucking office now." Red rushing in to replace the white sheen of mortification.

* * *

In the darkness deep breathing echoed. A flipper broke the centuries old sand. *We are called, the others must awake before it is too late.*

* * *

Charlie limped up behind Carol as she lay sun-tanning on Agate Beach on Haida Gwaii. "Nice tan. Heard you were here on holidays."

Carol jumped. "Hate it when you do that." Squinting, she yanked herself upright in her deckchair and peered over her dark sunglasses. "I didn't expect to see you on the islands. Although with your woo-woo stuff I might have figured I'd run into you sooner or later."

"Good to see you too, Carol. What drags you out here?" He hadn't seen her since they worked on solving the death of Vancouver's mayor last year.

"You hooked me. Decided I gotta see more of this place. And let me guess, I'm presuming this is probably a business call, since you're a bit over dressed for the beach." She looked him up and down over her sun-glasses realizing it was the same getup he wore then, probably was like Einstein who kept ten same outfits of everything in his closet. No, with Charlie, probably just the same one.

"Yeah, this is my office suit now." Charlie referred to his usual get up of seen-better-days denim. "I got hired by the Federal Government to be a paid Elder for the Prince Rupert Penitentiary."

"What? Were they mad?"

"No, I was the only one that applied. It seemed the other applications got lost."

Carol shook her head. "I've heard this story before. Lost by, let me guess, cousins of yours."

"Big family. We don't see each other much, but we're tight. Man, it's hot out here. Their last Elder died, more aptly was murdered, although I think the pen don't like that idea and are trying everything they know to get it signed off as what the WCB call 'a work related incident'. Covers all sorts of wrongdoing that title."

"Which, unless someone finds three knives in his back or several bullet holes, it is, and the police involvement ceases."

"Got that from the no-humour jail guard and a little bird that whispered it in my ear."

"A little bird whispered in your ear? That someone was murdered? Man, you hang out with a strange crowd. But then I already know that."

"Yeah, little bird, not you-know-who-giant-raven-type-bird, built like a triple-stacked burger, but sparrow sized. One of those woo-woo things of mine that you talk about was disturbed by something that happened at the supposed accident. Whatever is happening is sending physic shockwaves through the unknown world, as you'd probably call it, and the authorities won't let me near the scene. The disturbance happened in a native sweat lodge out on the back grounds, only some of the suspects involved are female. While I've got access to the men I can't enter the women's prison."

"They won't let you near the scene until it is ruled either a WCB incident or the coroner warrants there's enough evidence to open a homicide investigation." Carol knew where this was going. "So let me guess. You want me to cut my holiday short because a sparrow whispered in your ear and go to a penitentiary full of women to investigate a murder? Many of whom would just as soon blink and either kill me for being a cop, make goggle eyes at me or just out-and-out rape me?"

"Well, you're good at summing things up. Sharp cookie, Ms. Ainsworth. You did say you owe me a favour as I did save your, what do the gangstas on TV call it? Oh yeah, your white skinny ho ass. Which by the way is starting to burn. You need some higher SPF or some of my herbal cream."

Carol reached for her pack of smokes. "I've tried your herbal remedies. Bear-sweat, weasel pee and oak-tree pumice. Thanks, but I'll stick to the drugstore products. At least they have a money back guarantee." Carol remembered the large burl along Rawlings Trail in Stanley Park that, if you caught it just right, looked like the face of an old woman. Or at least to everyone else it was a burl with an old woman's face in it. She knew it was the living witch called the Lure trapped inside. It still gave her the creeps to think how close to death she came. She would have died if it wasn't for Charlie, in their last and, she thought at the time, only adventure together. *I'm not really thinking what I'm thinking, am I? Why didn't I bring a flask of wine with me or at least a mickey of whiskey?*

"Ah what the heck. I was getting bored anyway, already hung out up at Rosespit. Wanted to chat with my mom's spirit up there, but couldn't hook up with her. Need to work on that woo-woo stuff of yours some more." She paused and shook her head. "I know I'm going to regret what I'm about to say, but okay. And after this we're even. I can't be seen to be constantly talking to an old native man dressed forever in the same clothes. People will begin to think we're a team, or, heaven forbid, an item."

Charlie waited for Carol as she collected her things together. A couple with kids in tow walked by, all were staring at Charlie sweating away in his jeans and jean jacket. One of the children, a rotund girl of about twelve, was eating an ice cream cone. She frowned at the older man and stuck her tongue out. "Smelly Indian."

"Rude little girl." Charlie waved his cane and a stick that was lying in the sand lifted between the girl's shins and sent her flying. She tripped and fell face first, mashing ice cream and sand all over her face.

"Deal. We're even after this." Carol giggled as the girl screamed, spitting sand.

"Oh dear." Charlie walked on and said as he passed the couple, "You know its bad luck to take any agates and sand away from here, even ingested. Native legend, just like the ones in Hawaii regarding Pele', their fire goddess. She brings bad luck to anyone that takes away her sand and agates. I'd make sure you wash her mouth out, with soap preferably. Sand isn't good for the digestion anyways. Good day." He smiled as he passed.

The girl kept spitting sand and ice cream from her mouth. "He did it! He made me trip. Stinky old ..."

Charlie gave her a nasty glare. The girl decided to shut up.

"Now, you were just clumsy. I've told you before to watch where you're going. He wasn't even near you at the time," her mother scolded.

"But I know he ..."

"Enough! Get in the car now!" her dad yelled, "serves you right for being rude to your elders."

"See, my work precedes me." He walked with a swagger.

Carol looked quizzically at Charlie as they walked towards her car. "Did you do something to that girl back there?"

"My dad always told me to never piss off certain people in your life; your doctor, lawyer, a police officer or your shaman."

"Don't think he said shaman, probably minister."

"You didn't know my dad."

Carol laughed. "And now I know why you don't cheese off shamans."

Charlie laughed back. "Come to think of it, he might have said minister."

Chapter Two

He who tried to communicate with me, knew of a bird of metal. It flies with the excrement of the ancients in its bowels. It devours the ancients to fly? How is this possible? And humans inside. Living inside its belly? What kind of world is out there? I read writing on its wing, CE438571. I know letters, my language. I can communicate.

I reach out to speak to it.

* * *

James stared at his buzzer as it rang. "Who is it?

"Carol Ainsworth to see you, sir."

"See her in."

James rose to shake her hand. "Carol Ainsworth? The same Carol Ainsworth Detective in the Vancouver Police force? The Carol Ainsworth that cracked the Hell's Angels' crime spree and solved the murder of your mayor? Also involved in the cracking of the fake totems set up in Stanley Park?"

"Yes, to all of that. Wow, how is it you know all of this?"

"Just looking at your file because of one Charlie Stillwaters that we happen to have currently employed with us. The Charlie Stillwaters mentioned in some of the reports associated with those cases. I must admit I didn't know who he was until I read your file. I do like to know the background of the people that are coming to work with me or pop in for a visit out of the blue. I'm surprised he didn't put his association with you and the Vancouver Police Department in his resume. All one line of it."

"Modest guy. Environmentally conscious as well, doesn't like wasting paper. Carol smirked.

"I'd say a few things about him, but modest wouldn't be one of them."

Carol sat down. "Try exasperating."

"So why are you here, Detective?" James cut to the chase.

"Charlie asked me to help him investigate the death of Ken Benson, your last Elder on duty, who died under mysterious circumstances."

"Incorrect. He was involved in what we are hoping is about to be classed as a work related incident by the WBC investigators. The family, as you can guess, would like closure and some kind of settlement, as would we. This has caused a lot of unrest with the native population which will only grow as the days go on."

"Ah, that is what I hate about BC Criminal Law, everything at work is considered a 'work related incident' unless proven otherwise. However you are misinformed. This will not be signed off until the police have investigated and it could be some weeks for anyone to become available so I'm here to do you a big favour. I've called my boss and the powers that be and said I'd be willing to take on this investigation at least for the remainder of my vacation. My boss, lovely bastard of a chap, figured if I want to wreck my holidays, I can go right ahead."

"You can't do that."

"Why wouldn't you want me to? Surely you don't want to see a murderer go unpunished? Anyway I've already done it. I've already had a quick perusal of the crime scene photos and autopsy report. My boss had them e-mailed to me as soon as I was given the go-ahead and I do have severe misgivings about it being an accidental 'work related incident' hence me offering to give up my vacation. My own M.E. is looking over the autopsy for me as we speak. Now we'll see if someone found with their head bashed in is just 'a work related incident'."

"What are you talking about? He passed out and fell against the rocks, killing himself," James growled.

"Yes, that's what someone, maybe the WCB, want us to think. However the crime scene photos have given me a red flag and even your own M.E. hasn't ruled out foul play. Death was definitely blunt force trauma to the temple and this could be head-to-rock but just as easily rock-to-head, and I intend to find out exactly which. Someone was obviously happy just to think it was an accident and I wouldn't like to think what would happen to anybody that had misled WCB."

James looked hard at her.

"I think we may well have a murderer on the loose here and there's a good possibility this could happen again. How much more upset do you think it would cause if it does?"

James stared at her with hardened eyes. It was obvious he didn't want to back down but he knew he had no choice. Damn. He had so been hoping this would go so long without investigation the fuss would die down and it could be quietly swept under the carpet.

"As you probably know, I got special funding to perform sweats on this site due to the large native population. Opening a police investigation could endanger that and cause even more unrest by upsetting the inmates more than they already are. Worst day for a warden is having to deal with a riot so here's what I'm willing to do. I'll set you up as a prison employee IE guard, with all the necessary protocols. You look into this and if we find the evidence that there is wrongful doing here then we open the file as a homicide investigation. I don't want to upset his family as they are already in the belief that his death was an accident. Can you imagine the crap if we open this up thinking he's been murdered and find out he wasn't?"

"Okay, agreed. Good idea actually. Best to be sure before we tell the family anything else. However, as there were male and female inmates in that sweat lodge, I'm gonna need Charlie's help here. He can investigate the men and I will deal with the women. Lucky you've already hired him, isn't it? The sooner he and I can leave, the sooner this penitentiary can get back to normal and maybe I can even get back to my holidays."

He squeezed his eyes closed and took a couple of deep breaths. "Ms. Ainsworth. I run a tight prison. I've enough trouble keeping the inmates civil and I have nothing to do with any possible misleading of WCB. What I told you about him hitting his head is all I know. There's been a lot of unrest since the incident, especially since Ken was an ex-con, which you might not have known. I know there has to be an investigation at some point so I guess it's best to get it over with."

"No time like the present; how can I say this? Boss."

"Mr. Braithwaite to you. God you're a bitch. But that's probably why you're successful. But I do like a lady with balls or guts."

"You were probably wanting to say vagina."

"And get busted for sexual harassment? Not on your life. Now get to work and find my killer, if that's what you believe I have here."

"Okay. First I want to see the crime scene and if I bump into him shall I say 'hi' to Charlie from you?"

James glared darkly at her. "Get out."

"I do think he's right though, you should pick snazzier ties." She smiled as she left his office. Yup, as Charlie said, wound a little too tight and probably doesn't get much at home. Which currently was more than she was getting.

* * *

It walked along the shore.

I have counted every rock on this beach twice. I know every blade of grass, every totem that sits waiting. And I wait. Only why? Why am I waiting? Why am I alone?

* * *

"You've never worked before?" Carol said as she entered his office. She stared pointedly at the largely blank sheet of paper that was Charlie's resume. He looked up at her, he had been busy reading from the stack of documents sitting on the desk before him.

"Well, I'm a shaman. You know, live-off-the-land type. Help little animals fight oppression, the lack of nuts and the Freedom of Planting Act."

"The what?"

"The Freedom of Planting Act. It gives squirrels, chipmunks and even crows and ravens the right to plant fallen nuts wherever they desire."

Carol shook her head and smiled. "Can't say I've missed this inane banter of yours. But really, never had a real paying job before? How is this possible in our day and age?"

"I've had a few small jobs, fishing, selling jack pine mushrooms, got paid in cash. Darn Japanese are crazy, they'll pay nearly a thousand dollars a pound for the stuff. And they eat sushi, raw fish, yuck." Charlie wrinkled his nose. "Good to see you too Carol, I knew you were a person of your word."

Carol scratched at her shoulder where the sunburn hurt the worst. She hated him being right most of the time. "I thought you were a native, eat wild roots, live off the land. Smoke salmon."

"Yeah, but this is the twenty-first century. We've got electricity. Cooked, deep fried, breaded, now we're talking. Raw! Hell, haven't you heard of fish lice? They'll eat you alive from the inside out. That's it. I can't read anymore. If I knew I had to read this much, I'd have thought twice about getting hired. "Charlie got up and headed out the door of his office, chucking down the wad of paper before him.

"Hey, where you going?"

"Cafeteria, see if old Sandy will do me up a smoked salmon sandwich. Talking about food gets a guy hungry. Are you coming?"

Carol decided to join him. "You can't seriously be telling me you rerouted all of the applications so they'd have to accept yours?"

"Okay, so I won't tell you." Charlie laughed as he tapped his cane down the hallway.

"How did you tamper with the federal mail? Oh, let me guess."

"Nephews and uncles." They said at the same time.

"You're getting it."

Carol groaned. He either had great balls to pull off this kind of grandiose lunatic kind of stunt or dumb shit ass luck. Probably mainly the latter, she muttered to herself, remembering the incident earlier in the year with the smuggling out of the deceased shaman's remains into Stanley Park that Charlie had arranged by another of his 'nephews'. But she knew this, if he thought the man was murdered, he most likely was. Now they had to find just cause. "Okay take me out to the sweat lodge after we eat."

* * *

My breath chills in the dawn's air, mixing with the stillness. I shake the seawater from my pelt and tread inland as the shore laps gently behind me. It has been a long time since my kind have walked on this earth. But the time has come to end the slumber. I stop, voices echo in the mornings awakening.

"Derek, I think it went this way."

"Ah come on Tom. I think you've had one beer too many. You missed the deer completely."

"Six isn't too many and I know I winged him. Come on."

Intrigued, I glide through the bushes wondering what kind of humans are these speaking in a language I don't recognize. Nearby is the scent of fresh blood, a wounded deer. I remember that delicious smell. I lick my lips and edge closer, a branch cracks underneath.

They both spin in my direction. Thunder erupts from their metallic rods in a horrible voice and more metal whizzes through the air, thumping into a tree behind me. I react in defense. I shouldn't, the humans don't know we're here, but I must defend myself from these thunder weapons of destruction. Where did they come from? Have the humans evolved so much since our last being here? They bear strange dress of unnatural fibres and no longer shoot wood through bent sticks.

Claws dig in and I launch myself through the air, deep growls spring from within.

"What the fu…" *is all one gets to utter as my claws tear his insides out. Warm intestines and blood splatter the ground. The other falls backwards as delicious smell of fresh blood fills the air. How I've missed that aroma.*

Its thunder weapon discharges and searing agony hammers my left shoulder. I rake the screaming one's throat, ending its pain. More wonderful redness erupts everywhere. But I can't feed on this one as my shoulder cries out in agony and my own blood splatters the ground.

"What in God's name is that? Hang on Tom, I've got to reload."

More thunder retorts from the metal rod's mouth and narrowly misses me. I must leave to heal. I cannot defeat this weapon it holds. I have underestimated the humans. I glare deep into the face of this one. ***Derek.*** *I call out in my mind to him.*

He stares stunned at me, unbelieving. I inhale his scent. I will return to hunt him for what he has done to me. We can't be found out, not before we eliminate the one who awoke us. I lop through the dense bush as he recovers his shock and more metallic projectiles whistle by, tearing apart vegetation, but little else. I have never run in fear from anything and won't again. I will return as I dive into the cold sea water shifting my form.

* * *

Carol stood beside the sweat lodge smoking a cigarette. "Yeah, talk me into some crazy things old man. You kill my vacation to investigate a murder in a pen full of women that would like me for only one thing; as in stick their hands down my pants, or beat me senseless, and then instead of being on a hot beach, I end up investigating a room full of hides. Sweaty ones at that."

"That's why it's called a sweat lodge. Hey, some of the prison guards look quite hunky. Even the female ones. You never know, could find a good date here."

"Yeah, the only ones that I seem to have attracted so far are the hunky females. I bet there's probably a lot of that same sex thing going on around here."

"Well they're in jail but still get the urge."

"Ever do it with a woman, Charlie?" Carol just couldn't even visualize him in bed with one. *Let alone seeing him naked... Nah, not going there*. She shook her head.

"I never thought you'd be the type to ask."

"Ever think about it? Hey, if we're supposed partners I gotta ask, get to know you." *On the other hand, sometimes the less you know about your partner the better.*

"Nope straight and narrow."

"Yeah, same, hot dog material only and yourself?"

"Much the same. Don't butter my bread on both sides of the slice."

"Yeah, pure straight. Glad we got that in the open, but if that's the case who's the lucky lady. Don't see a ring on your finger except that black onyx one. Which I believe is for friendship."

"Calming as well." Charlie sat quiet for a long moment as he turned the ring on his finger. "Given to me by Lucy. She died of illness in my arms when I was twenty-two. We'd just met the year before. Her favourite artist and mine is Roy Orbison. I'll always remember his song, Crying, was playing in the background as she died. It was because of that I decided to become a shaman. I couldn't save her, but thought if there was some way to visit her, on the other side so to speak, I would. I also pledged my undying love to her. I'm a man of my word."

"And no one since."

"Nope. The equipment is kinda healed over since then. No desire for another. I became a shaman after that. If I can't save her then I'll save some others."

"Admirable man you are Charlie Stillwaters."

"Nuts is more what I am. I coulda got lucky so many times. There's more than a few lonely gals out there I've bumped into at the grocery store or out hiking the backcountry." He laughed.

"You meet horny single women out hiking? Man, got any good places I could bump into a hot hunky fireman type of male?" Carol chuckled back as she ground out her cigarette and they entered the sweat lodge, the ceiling so low neither could stand upright.

He looked at her appalled by her upfront attitude.

"I'm not pious, just a bit afraid. It's a lonely world being a detective, not many guys want to know someone who lives on the edge of possibly being shot or killed every day. But as I get older, if I meet a good looking guy, and we go out on a date, I do allow him to get to a homerun faster. Thinking if he ain't Mr. Right he might as well clang all my bells. Beats watching 'Sex And The City' reruns."

He opened his eyes at that revelation. "Thanks for the honesty. I can see you're obviously less frustrated than me."

"Are you frustrated? Must be hard to not want to do it one way or another?"

"No, part of my training gets me past the need for; how do you say it politely?"

"Release."

"Yup, interesting conversation to be having inside a sweat lodge." Carol shook her head. "You're an interesting character Charlie."

"Hey, if you want interesting, let me tell you about my Roy Orbison record collection."

"Records? You mean those large black CD's? Didn't know they still made those. Yeah, I'll pass on that one, I'm more of a U2 type of person."

She lifted the flap to the sweat lodge so that some light, and fresh air could enter.

"Hey, vinyl is making a comeback I hear. Can't quite get the same background depth of music, they tell me on those silver Frisbee things. U2? Didn't know any of the people on the German submarines released any kind of music. But I could recite some baseball stats on the Montreal Expos."

She smiled. "I'll pass on that one as well. Now enough of the chit-chat." Carol looked around at the central fire pit area. The stones were still in place but were now, obviously, cold.

"Drats! Back to work is it boss lady?"

* * *

A dark figure from the edge of the forest next to the pen watched the two moving around inside the sweat lodge for a few minutes before slowly slinking back into the darkness at the edge of the woods.

* * *

Carol grabbed her notebook and began to jot down notes. Charlie scratched his head, watching her. "What are you doing?"

"Notes, and lots of them. First rule of a crime scene investigation, even if the scene is a week old, first impressions are critical. Along with pictures and measurements." She pulled out a tape measure.

"Pull it to the end." Carol ordered.

"I'm measuring this why?"

"Because it's evidence. Do as I say and quit asking questions. I'm in charge. I never ask why you carry a bag full of medical herbs around, do I?"

Charlie looked at her. "Medicine pouch, it's a medicine pouch. Okay you do your job and I'll do mine. No questions."

Carol looked around, her head lost deep in jotting down notes. *We'll see how long thy stillness of lips lasts.* The dimensions of the lodge lent itself to more than enough room for more than ten people to be inside, which meant they weren't elbow to elbow. She checked the height, noting that at five-foot no one except Snow White's bedmates could have stood up properly.

"Man, I think that you whites have poor memories and waste a lot of trees on this kind of thing." He watched her scribbling away in her pad.

"I didn't think analytical investigation was your kind of thing. So did you notice what I noticed in my supposed waste of time jotting down notes and killing one spruce tree and half an ounce of lead?"

"That at a crime scene you get writing cramps and are rather boring?"

"No. I thought shamans were observant. So did you notice what I noticed?"

Charlie screwed up his face and scratched his head with the end of his cane. "Nope and I've already tried the old zipper down hotdog gimmick yesterday, which doesn't work so well with females."

"Yeah, no hotdog. How about the gap in the pile of stones?"

"What gap?"

She pointed to the depression in the soil where another stone may have lain. She took a couple of close pictures. "It is possible it could have been dislodged when the inmates left the lodge. However it could just be a red herring."

"Herring? We back to that sushi stuff again?"

"No, silly. A red herring is what you think is a clue but isn't and only serves to mislead you. However would be handy if we could find it, even if just to rule it out."

Charlie stared, wrinkling his nose again at the thought of raw fish. "I knew there was a reason I hired you to help me." It was odd that he had been so lost in trying to pick up psychic residue that he hadn't thought to notice what was right in front of his face. "I must admit I'm wrong and you've caught me in the opposite of when we first met."

"Ah, I remember those the famous words, 'If you weren't white you'd see all the clues that are around you.'" Charlie nodded quietly, remembering his quick cockiness at their first meeting in Stanley Park where the mayor of Vancouver had been brutally slain. Where he'd said the same thing except using native in the context of white. "Now from what I understand natives believe in the four cardinal points of the compass." Charlie nodded in agreement. "And always the sign of leadership comes from the East spreading West and up and down so… I believe Ken Benson would have been sitting about here." Carol indicated a space opposite to where the stone may have been missing.

Charlie thought a moment. "How would you know that?"

"I read about traditional sweat lodges on the ferry ride over. Again it's important to know as much about a situation as possible in case it lends itself to the investigation and I discovered this fact. So that tells me the suspect, if there is one, knew Benson would be sitting here and that the suspect is most likely native as well."

"Why is that important?"

"Because in the gloomy light of the lodge at the time you would need to know where your mark would be so you didn't off the wrong person."

"Man, that's amazing deductions. All that from a few notes and powers of observation. I will never bug you about note taking again, well except at dinner. You can't write and eat at the same time. Gives you ulcers."

"However from the crime scene photos," Carol continued, deciding not to rise to the bait this time, "Ken was laying here, slumped over, probably dead or at least severely incapacitated before his head hit the ground. Highly unlikely he managed to move after his head was hit. So if his body was here," Carol pointed to where he had been found "but the stones were here," she indicated the fire pit some distance away "how did he fall, hit his head on the stones, and then fall down dead or incapacitated some six or eight feet back." Carol busied herself with the tape measure again to get the accurate figure, indicating to Charlie to assist.

"So you know what this means?" Carol continued.

He scratched his head. "That I've got to buy a measuring tape, pen and a pad?"

"No, it means our Elder was more than likely murdered." She shook her head and whispered under her breath. "Like someone else I'd like to have done in."

"What little old me? Come on, you got to say I've made your life interesting."

"Interesting? I'm supposed to be relaxing on a beach sun-tanning, hoping that some hunk of a man, lifeguard, general stud type muffin would see me. Say, something like 'hey good looking want a date or a quick roll in the hay'. No, instead I'm on my knees inside some smelly native sweat lodge in the back of a prison. Few would call this interesting, humourous or I'm just a sucker for punishment."

"Do I sense a little resentment? I think you could use a good shrink."

"Good shrink? What I need is a good cattle truck. How's your rhyming slang?" She laughed.

Charlie squinted as he tried to work it out in his head. "Oh, my. Did I mention I hate suckers? Chocolate bars though, now that's a different matter."

"Now we know more what we're looking for we need to get the CSIs back in – some that know what they're doing. Who was here before? High-school students? We'll also need to extend the crime scene area, see if we can find that stone, although admittedly that will take some doing. If this was planned rather than spur-of-the-moment the murderer sure knew what he or she was doing. Murder weapon already easily to hand and not at all suspicious. I'll call the warden to make sure he continues to have this place under twenty-four hour guard."

"Good idea, I like it. You get to put more yellow tape up now?"

"Yes, that means I've got to put up more yellow police tape to widen the perimeter."

"It's going to make me cry you know."

"I've heard of crying at funerals, but crime scenes? You're one strange man, Charlie Stillwaters."

"No, reminds me of the first time we met. I get all teary eyed and everything."

They'd met at the taped off area in Stanley Park where Vancouver's mayor had been murdered, late at night.

"I think I should be the one that's crying. It took me over a month to find you in Vancouver and I still get nightmares when I think of those maggots raining down on me." Carol shivered. Charlie had led her to the discovery of the mayor's daughter's body trapped inside an ancient cedar in Stanley Park. When she reached up and dislodged the rocks holding the body in place, all the maggots and grubs feeding off the body rained down on her.

"Well, you know the journey is always better than the destination." He snickered.

"The only destination I want right now is back to sun-tanning on the beach and less I journey with you the better." She shrugged her shoulders in shivering disgust.

"Hey, you're breaking my heart, and here I was getting all sentimental over our first date."

"Date? That'll never happen. The only dates you'll get from me is a pound of dried Moroccan over the back of the head."

"Well, I see you're beginning to get my sense of humour. Can I help you with your yellow tape?" As they exited the lodge Charlie turned to stand facing it, away from the forest. Earlier as they were joking around he got that internal shiver that he was being watched. The sensation he called his Spidey sense from the old Spiderman movies. Over his shoulder to the left he sensed it again. I was right. There is something out there watching me, or us. He spun around and caught a flash of light. Gone.

* * *

I try to awake the shaman, I must reach out. Only he is dead, killed, by who?

And who?

Who I am?

* * *

Charlie sat down next to Thomas Johnson, or the Griz as he now called himself the next day. "Hey, Big Mountain Grizzly. How's it hanging?" Charlie smiled. They were the only two at the table. Thomas reached out and plunged his fork into Charlie's stack of potatoes. "Good thing I brought extra."

"Only you can call me Big Mountain. To everyone else, I'm just Griz."

"Short and to the point. I like men of action. Have a piece of chicken, one only, I brought an extra for you. I'd hate to see how many calories it takes just to lift those arms every day."

"Bloody lot more than they feed me around here." He pushed the biggest piece of chicken onto his plate.

"So how's it going today?"

"The usual. Bell goes off, guards wake me up, let me out. I get to pee, and eat. If anyone looks in my direction I scowl, they leave me alone and I get to sit here feeling sorry for myself. Been this way for two years and most likely another six." He devoured the chicken in two large gulps. "Although in the cell next to Duncan and his lover Jamie." He growled that sentence, obviously not enamoured with that kind of sexuality, which Charlie gathered probably happened a lot around here. "They mentioned that strange bloke from the sweat."

"Which strange bloke?"

"You know, Bryan Samuels. He's not all there. A few nuts missing inside." He twirled his fingers around beside his head. "He's been muttering a lot at night and Duncan swears it's some foreign language, German or whatever. They also hear a lot of scribbling, like he's writing on the walls. Me, I keep to myself. The guards go in and wash it all off every morning, I'm told. Any more potatoes?" He glanced in Charlie's direction. The shaman nodded and let Griz shovel the rest of the potatoes into his plate.

"Really you should learn to chew your food, hard on the gut. Can't digest meat properly in such large chunks."

"Who the hell are you? My mother?" He growled deeply, obviously not used to being told off by anyone.

"Well, speaking of. I've put out there the paperwork and it seems we've got a response back, from a Florence Sanderson. Claims she's been looking for a son that was taken from her and put into residential school in Mission, BC."

He stared, his fork fell out of his fingers. A single tear immediately snaked its way down his face. Quickly he wiped it away with his meaty hands. "If you're fucking with me, I'll bust you up so bad, you'll need a wheelchair not a cane, old man." Griz leaned into Charlie. He'd meant every word.

"Didn't I say I was here to help you?"

"They all say that." He growled deeply, his anger on the edge of exploding. "Do you know why she abandoned me and never got me. Ever? Bitch." His teeth grit.

"Look, I'm off to see her this weekend. Don't know anything else so don't get your hopes up. Could be someone else's mother."

Sneered. "Thanks for the food but you better go now."

Charlie could see the rage brewing inside. "Yeah, thanks for the tip." He quietly got up and walked from the canteen. That man had so much suppressed anger it was no wonder he was in here for attempted murder. If there was some way to help him, he'd swear he'd find it.

* * *

I shake my head and try to communicate. Again and again. Only? I've killed it. The bird of metallic. Watching it crash to the earth.

I remember now, I had others in my life.

But I am not nice. That is why I am here. I am bad thing. I should be alone.

Chapter Three

Whump. Whump.

Something heavy hit the ground. Feet scrambling.

Charlie opened his eyes, concentration broken on his meditation. Scant minutes later the pen's alarms were going off and James' voice came over the PA system. "This is a lock down. Everyone back in your cells. Now. Repeat. This is a lockdown."

"How is a guy supposed to get any meditating done around here with all that racket going on?" He got up and walked over to the area where he spotted several guards stuffing small saran wrapped cylinders into plastic garbage bags. "What is going on?" He asked one of the guards.

"Every few days, someone delivers, via mortar or bazooka, a load of heroin."

"You aren't kidding?"

"No, sorry. The procedure is to lockdown the prison, grab what we can on the ground and begin searching every prisoner for more, then incinerate the stuff. Only last week the dope was loaded with Fentanyl and we had three prisoners die of overdose."

"Really," Charlie replied. "So you're not kidding me, smuggling in via bazooka, what ever happened to the old days of using a cake or slipping the guards a fiver?. I don't care for drugs, they steal away the soul and destroy the will to live your life's purpose. Kinda like a succubus, basically suck all good away and kill you in the end."

The guard looked at him like he couldn't believe what he just heard from the lips of this disheveled looking unwashed native man.

"Oh, and they really bugger up my beauty sleep, not that I need it. I've been told I'm a dead ringer for the soccer dude, Christian Ronaldo."

The guard laughed. "The closest thing you've got to Ronaldo is skin colour. But what's an old man going to do about it when we can't catch them. A mortar can deliver a payload up to half a mile away."

Charlie pursed his lips. "We'll see about that." He stormed off. "Time for some lunch anyways."

* * *

Carol stood in the aisle of the small grocery store. She'd found a studio apartment with kitchenette to rent for the next couple of weeks at a reasonable price just off the waterfront of Prince Rupert.

Absentmindedly she loaded her cart with the usual food requirements, coffee, potato chips, cinnamon toast and whiskey. She'd already grabbed a couple of cartons of smokes. Dealing with that whacked out shaman, she knew she'd be smoking more than her usual amount. *So much for a holiday, I'll probably get emphysema thanks to Charlie. That and a few hangovers.*

At the mention of her somewhat named partner, she caught a man offhandedly staring at her. Long dark hair, piercing black eyes, he seemed to be shopping, but more watching and following her. *Odd duck*. She decided to play along and instead of heading out to the checkout, looked at a few more items to see if indeed he was checking her out. He seemed to stay near the end of the aisle, but his eyes never left her. *Yeah, okay, I've a small town stalker or at least an admirer. Not having had a good romp with any male lately had started to make the advances of some of the dykes in the jail begin to look more appealing. Except for the fact I couldn't lick anything fishy and the thought of pubes on my tongue makes me gag.* She accepted the fact long ago that being a copper meant either finding the right kind of man, probably another law officer or enjoying the use of her best friend, Roger, her battery operated nightmate. Oh, need some batteries as well. Okay, I've had enough of mister dark and creepy. He was dressed in a long trench coat. *That's odd in itself in this heat.*

Carol turned and began to go in his direction. He picked up a container of canned tuna and appeared to be reading the label. As she was to pass by him, she stopped. "Is that good tuna?" she asked.

He sputtered, obviously caught off guard. "Ah, no. foul. Packed in water, can be quite stinky." He turned and glared at her. His dark eyes seeming to penetrate straight into her. "Hate stinky waters."

"Thanks, I'll pass." Carol pushed quickly past him. The face wasn't nearly the same, but she remembered the voice. It was the same cold dark voice, but a different man that had followed her in the bookstore on Haida Gwaii last year. She turned down the next aisle and began to walk quickly down the row. *No, damnit. I'm checking him out. It can't be him.*

She spun around, leaving her cart. Hand on her badge. *I'll apprehend him and ask a few questions.* The vague reference to Stinkwaters he used last time in slamming Charlie.

Carol looked up and down the end of the row. There was no one in the aisle, only his shopping cart. *What the... ?*

She quickly moved along all eight aisles of the small store. She was virtually the only one in the store, other than a lady that had eaten far too many chips. *Okay I'm putting my chips back and buying salad.* She grabbed her cart and headed for the checkout. As she placed her groceries on the counter she asked, "Did a dark haired man wearing a trench coat just leave here in a hurry?"

The middle aged lady looked at her oddly. "No, just you and Beatrice, buying her usual chips and pop are in the store today."

"You sure? Because I was just talking to a man in a trench coat."

"Lady, I can see everything from those curved mirrors. No man has been in here in the last half an hour." The woman pointed to the large convex mirrors above her.

"What? Okay explain the cart full of food in the tinned aisle."

The lady looked up at her mirrors. "What grocery cart?"

Carol spun around and walked down the row to the aisle in question. It was devoid of people and carts. "What?"

She slowly walked back to the cashier. "Yeah, sorry. It's been a long day. Need a smoke and a good drink."

"Or three." The lady laughed.

"Or three," she agreed.

* * *

"Madness merely depends on which end of the knife blade you're staring at," Charlie said to the native man waving the knife in his direction. Silver glinted evilly under the neon lights.

"Don't fuck with me, Shaman, or I'll gut you like a fish." The native man threatened. He'd bumped into Charlie as he'd strolled in from the outside. How the man got a knife, he didn't know and where he got his headful of anger was a bigger mystery. But a good reason why he was here in this jail.

"Now I do believe knives aren't allowed on the premises. That means I'm going to have to report you. Could mean another few months in solitaire. Great card game, by the way, but I guess you've never played it.

Simple rules, and as my French brothers in Quebec say, only need one homme," As the native approached him, Charlie glared into his eyes. "I see you probably don't play it much as there's a few too many inside you for that to happen, isn't there?"

The man's eyes moved back and forth as if there was an internal struggle going on, but the one holding the knife remained. "I'm going to slice you up old man." He said, a sneer etching his face.

The warden stared down at the scene from the floor above the commotion. He'd been called out from his office by Jenkins one of his guards.

"Shall I call in the guards before he's stabbed?" Jenkins asked. "And I believe its pronounced 'om', not 'homee'."

James whispered back, "Shh, I'm just curious to see if he doesn't get sliced up. Charlie is pretty confident looking. I heard what he did with Thomas. Let's see if that was plain shit luck or not." He paused. "But be ready to call in the guards if this goes sideways. I think we should hold back and see what our new Elder is capable of. After all, what's one more death to file in the paperwork anyways." He smiled, Jenkins already knew he had an intense dislike for the cocky shaman.

"Well, I do hope you've washed that blade. I've been known to pick up colds and infections rather easily. As a young boy I stepped on a rusty nail. Foot swelled up, couldn't walk for two weeks. My grandmother had to make me a poultice from some foul smelling substance. Essence of root and horse dung. Didn't know what was worse the swollen leg or the cow-patty swelling cure. That was probably the beginning of my career as a shaman. I figured I could make a much better smelling poultice and strike it rich in the herbal field."

"Shut up, old man. Just shut up," he yelled, more to himself than to Charlie, who watched the dance back and forth in his eyes. The one inside holding the knife was struggling to stay in control.

So he decided to push his luck and call him on it. "But if you were going to cut me, I'd reckon you'd do it first and not talk me to death. A true warrior goes into battle sword first. Bullshitters and bullies like to feel big and powerful. Instill fear. It's a drug to them, gets them over their insecurity and lack of confidence. And like I said earlier, true madness, well that just depends on which end of the blade you're staring at and you ain't mad, and truly no warrior. So I reckon that makes you a bullshitter or bully." Charlie smiled widely as he stared deep into the man's eyes. Something inside changed as his gaze shifted. "Now that we've gone full circle you've only got to ask yourself one question, 'little Tommy Blackfeathers.' What are you truly scared of?"

He stared at the shaman as his face dropped and stood there, hand shaking. "How did you know my name? No one has called me that in a long time." Tears began to streak his face as it softened. He'd been found out.

He'd read his file yesterday. Tom Blackfeathers was one of the ones involved in both of the sweats. "So that begs me to ask the question, if I ain't scared of you, it's either because I'm madder than you are or I've a bigger weapon. Which leads to the next question, 'when he's done with me what orifice is he going to shove it up'?"

Tommy's eyes clouded. Tears struggled to stay back. Fear clawed away at his vision.

"You know about things being shoved up your orifice. Don't you, Little Tommy BlackFeathers?"

"Leave me alone, don't touch me. I'll do anything you want." Tears streamed down his face as he collapsed to his knees. A little boy from inside stared up at Charlie, trembling in terror.

"Drop the knife. I'm not a bully, I won't harm you. Not like the others. The ones that made you the way you are today." He'd seen some pretty horrifying things in his day. But Charlie couldn't imagine, nor wanted to, what this man went through as a boy. He'd heard many of the kids were sexually abused in the residential schools. He was so blessed that he never attended one.

"Can you help me?" Tears welled up in the eyes of a six year old frightened boy. "Please?"

"I ain't your folks. But I can help." The knife cluttered to the ground, he knew what he saw in the man's eyes wasn't good and this went far beyond anything he knew how to deal with. "That's why I'm here. To help. You've my word on that."

The warden stood watching, amazed, as the assembled crowd gasped. Charlie walked towards the kneeling prisoner and instead of kicking the knife away he fell to his knees as well and pulled the lad to his chest. Whispering encouraging words he stroked the dark hair of the prisoner that began to sob openly as Charlie hugged him.

"How the fuck did he do that?" James pulled Jenkins aside. "In his dossier there's no formal training on dealing with confrontational prisoners. No mention of recognizing people with split personality disorder. But somehow he knew of Tom's condition. I want to know how."

"None, sir."

"Okay, put a halt to the paperwork on hiring a new Elder. Whatever he's got is either luck or pure natural instinct. I dislike this man very much, everything about him offends me. But he's very good and maybe exactly what we need around here."

"You want to keep him, sir?"

"Yes. Bust up the crowd and get him in my office pronto. I want a few words alone with Mr. Stillwater. Now."

"Yes, sir."

* * *

Derek stood among the ones with uniforms and others dressed in white. The ones in uniform. *These here now were beings of order and justice similar to the ones in charge at the place with the stone walls. The reason I was awakened, to find the one that can't wake up.*

I watched them from the dense bush. They also carried thundersticks. The ones in white were measuring and marking everything before moving the already smelling remains of the dead one called Tom. Ones meant to clean up the scene, I supposed. Didn't matter, my shoulder throbbed but it was already nearly healed. Our kind had the natural ability to cure ourselves quickly. My tongue bade for the taste of my vengeance. Derek's blood.

"So you're saying you were attacked by a very large wolf and it gutted your friend." One of the humans spoke.

"Yes, only this is going to sound crazy. It didn't look like any wolf I'd ever seen before. It had something on its back, like a… a blowhole you'd find a whale or an orca. And attached to the back of its legs, something that looked like small appendages, like fins." *He named Derek, paused is if he didn't want to admit more disbelief.* "That, that wolf thing spoke. It said my name."

"What?"

"I know you're probably going to lock me in the loony bin. But just before it vanished, it spoke my name. I heard it in my head."

I wanted to burstfrom these bushes, and attack wildly all gathered.

We could not be known about. Not yet. I glanced again at the thunder-sticks on the hips of the uniforms. Maybe now wasn't the time? I waited, watching them wrap the body up and take it away. The hunger gnawed at me. I needed the taste of his blood on my tongue.

***Derek**. I whispered sweetly from my mind.* **Come to me**. *He turned as the last were leaving, listening to the winds and my calling.*

"Give me a moment. I'll be right back." Derek walked forward. *I watched one of the uniforms glance his way. The one he was just talking to.*

"Hang on, I can't leave you alone out here. The creature may still be about or other wild beasts attracted by the smell of blood and rotting corpse."

I let the two walk several feet towards the shore. Away from the safety of the others. Metallic machines mounted on circular rubbers moved away, foul noxious gas spewing from their lungs; only one remained. My vengeance would be satiated. I began to howl low.

"Did you hear that?"

The uniform ran his hand over his smaller thunder gun. "I did. What is that? A wolf?"

"I told you. It's some kind of weird creature I've never seen or heard of before."

Before either could move I stole from the brush and leapt. The uniform's body hit the ground as delicious hot blood sprayed upwards. I held his torn head in my jaws, the mouth still screaming, "watch out." *Wonderful hot blood spurted everywhere. Coating me like a delicious musk. I howled my delight to the sky, dropping the trophy.*

Derek stared stunned and ran into the brush as I crunched brain matter down my throat. I'd already planned the approach of my attack and knew he was cut off running away from help. Mine, all mine. Most stupendous. The time was due. I hunkered after him. Fear, sweet fear splattered the ground and threaded the air. The prey trembling before the hunter. I howled, it had been a long time since I've hunted and nothing brings greater satisfaction to a predator. I smiled and picked up my pace.

He stumbled, blood sprang free as his face and hands tore over bare rocks on the shore. Perfect, my pet. I leapt as he stood to face me. This would be quick, as I heard others running towards us. Too late, oh so too late. This one is mine. All mine.

Claws tore flesh apart as my jaws tore into the chest crushing past ribs. I ripped lungs free as thunder rippled in the air. They were coming, but it was too late. My fins entered the water as his blood and matter rained down through the salty waters. I licked bits of matter settling around me. It had been far too long since my last stalking. I smiled in enjoyment, for nothing is greater pleasure than sweet, terrible vengeance to the heart of the predator.

* * *

"Hello Governor." Charlie entered the warden's office trying to elicit a proper English accent, but he sounded more like the Geico Gecko after six beers.

James Braithwaite looked over his glasses at the smiling native and spoke in his usual posh sounding London straight-from-the-mouth-of-the-Queen's English accent, "Sit down Mr. Charles Stillwater."

Charlie looked about. "Are you referring to me, James? If you check my birth records you will see that the proper name is Charlie and ..."

James raised his voice, which normally had a very commanding deepness to it, sounding like Churchill commanding the English to defeat the Nazis during the Second World War "Sit down now, Mr. Charlie Still-water. Other than the impromptu meeting in the hallway yesterday, we haven't been properly introduced. I normally will meet with every one of my staff before they begin working here. It appears you have jumped the gun on me and have caught me somewhat unprepared."

Charlie sat down.

"I'll be honest, I have your termination papers drawn up and before me awaiting my signature. As soon as someone, anyone, with a decent resume applies you are out of here. Keep up the glib tongue and I'll have you out of here in seconds." He lied.

Charlie sat quietly deciding to quell his tongue a moment and listen before he told the warden how far he could stuff his job.

"Now, you've no formal training in your resume. But I caught that display earlier this afternoon, with Tom Blackfeathers. Most impressive. Not only did you not back down from a man brandishing a knife, you managed to recognize the fact he has split personality disorder and break his will as well. I also heard yesterday of the incident in the canteen where you managed to befriend prisoner 4532032, Thomas Johnson, and even gave him a nickname. This is unheard of, no one gets within three feet of that man. He'd as soon kill someone as smile at them. Not only did you make him smile, but you managed to break him down, befriend him and make him laugh. Again, all in the matter of a few minutes."

"You mean bad tempered, turn on a dime, good old Big Mountain Griz. Just getting to make a few buds around the place, thought we could sit down and have few heart to heart, mano to mano type chats and ask him what's the latest on breaking out of this joint? I hear on the down low, Jimmy, there's a lot of digging sounds being heard late at night in cell block eight."

"Very funny man you are Charlie. A little humour around here could be used, even by myself. So tell me a little about yourself. I want to know what you did and how you did it in those two situations. Or am I to assume that was pure gut instinct for someone facing death and about to be gutted. Also before we get off on the wrong understanding it's still James Braithwaite, Senior Warden. Sir, to you."

Charlie stared into the no nonsense eyes of the warden. "Well, Mr. Senior Warden, Sir James Braithwaite. I am a shaman and as such I use a lot spiritual techniques, things like the study of Quantum Holistic, Human Field Magnetic therapies and ..." He watched James' eyes grow large under his glasses and back flip through Charlie's empty resume.

"Where the hell does it say anything about this?"

"Nah, I'm just shitting ya. I caught that on TV the other night watching that curry dude, Ceepak Chop-em-up. Also read some of the stuff in your library. Interesting material down there, I might even take a few books home to read on weekends when I'm babysitting the nieces and nephews. Can't say I buy a lot of it, but interesting. I haven't asked where you keep the section with all the comic books. I do like a little more deep spiritual reading, like Archie and Jughead."

"Stop right there. I didn't ask you into my office to bullshit me or play me for a fool, CHARLIE!" He growled very loudly without moving a muscle. Charlie noticed the intense control this man had to contain himself, yet get his point across. "Now, start talking straight or I'll sign these papers and ship you the hell back from whatever mumbo jumbo hole you crawled out of. GET IT?"

Charlie nodded and stared at the warden a moment. "You know I didn't care for you when we first met and after that outburst I think I'm supposed to shit my drawers. But I'm beginning to grow some respect for you now. You've a tough job here James." He caught an eyebrow raise ever so slightly. "I think you've developed a very thick skin to keep it from getting to you in this place. You've grown a thick cover to guard your heart or to ..."

"Show that I care." The warden lifted his hand stopping Charlie from speaking further. He didn't intend to let that slip out. Composing himself he continued, "You are good, Charlie Stillwater, very good. No one else has cut through that veneer I put in front of myself or has to guts to try and that's one of your natural gifts, I assume by lack of information on this resume."

"Thanks. I see now that your arrogance is just a front. After all some-one has to whip the boys around here and unfortunately you're the lucky dominatrix of this federal dungeon and according to government regula-tions, let even allowed one lousy whip, leather, cat-tailed or not."

The warden smiled for the first time that Charlie had ever seen.

"I think part of that smart tongue of yours is also a way keeping your-self safe as well. I don't care for smartasses, I'll let you know right now. But if you want to stay working here we need a few understandings. First of all, I sign your paycheque, which means if I say Happy Birthday, you supply the cake and candles. Is that understood?"

"Yes, Sir. And may I say you are rather cute when showing who's in charge."

"Now, can the shit. Your job is to help the inmates and mine is to keep this place running as sanely as possible and within budget. So your salary based on your skill level will be pegged at whatever minimum it can be set at. Understand."

"You're keeping me?" Charlie straightened up.

"Don't know why, I've got a new batch of applications for your position in my email this morning. But Charlie Stillwater there is something about you that I like and trust. Call it guts, balls, or inbred honour, but that's what I need around here right now. Whatever shamanic training or learnings you've had I can't attest to, but I can see that you are very observant and have the ability to see the truth inside people. Most impressive for a raw talent."

Charlie blushed slightly.

"Now get out of my office and start dealing with all of those messed up guys out there before they end up killing each other. Oh, and speaking of death there's something I want you to see and tell me what you make of it. Meet me in the isolation ward in ten minutes. The day after the killing of your predecessor this prisoner went berserk and filled the walls of his cell with strange scribbles, and he's still doing it. I was going to have it washed down today, but I want you to look at it first."

"Aye aye Governor," he said in his best drunken Gecko voice. "Oh and do check your records, it is Charlie Stillwaters."

"What?" James glanced at his file of papers. He buzzed his assistant. "Jenkins, can you go through this file and verify Charlie Stillwaters' correct name. Damn it." He slammed down the phone as Charlie sauntered out.

Chapter Four

Charlie stared at the scribbles as he and the warden entered the cell while the man was taken out. "This was written by one of the inmates that was in the sweat lodge a day before the murder? Which one?"

"Bryan Samuels. He's normally quiet and reserved."

"His background?"

"Another raised in a residential school. Yes, apparently abused there. His file is on your desk. I've had Jenkins gather up all pertinent information about the ten inmates from the sweat so that you can read up on their pasts. Might help with finding out what happened."

"Ah, you really are such a charmer, James. I've a desk?"

"Yes, in your office."

"Oh yeah, forgot about that. How cool is that? My own office." Charlie twirled his cane about. "Do I have a list of everyone involved?"

"The list is on top. In addition all the other aboriginal inmates are in your files. But remember you're just the Elder and not a criminal investigator. We are just waiting for this to be signed off as a work related incident."

"Now James, don't be telling me porkies."

"Porkies?" queried James.

"Why James. I would have thought that ol' rhyming slang would be right up your particularly English street. Pork pies; lies. Therefore porkies. You know that I know that's not true and that it is being investigated by Vancouver's finest. In fact, as I also know you know, yours truly here is helping the good detective with her detecting!"

"I really don't see what use you'll be," James replied scathingly. He hated the fact that Detective Ainsworth, of all people, was investigating what he had hoped would just go away but he hated even more that this idiot was to be involved in it too.

"As a shaman I've investigated a lot of strange things like this and I've done things that would shake your religious beliefs to the core." Charlie glared along the walls, turning his and James' attention back to the scrawls on it. "I'm not an archelogy type of guy. I don't know what this writing is. But..." Charlie put his hand and nose to the wall and breathed deep. Sniffing. "I get timeless, ancient, very ancient. You may have something brewing here more than a mere murder."

"And I'm to trust a crazy old man who's hooked on a nonexistent baseball team, doesn't wash and smells walls?"

"Much! Doesn't wash much. And there is so much in evidence right in front of what your normal senses can't tell you. I get the spirit of whatever wrote this and it isn't our prisoner." He closed his eyes and inhaled again.

"Much. And talks in gibberish. But I've seen you in operation and as crazy as everyone around here will say, I'm beginning to really trust you."

"Beginning? When I'm done with this case, you'll be phoning Scotland Yard and telling them you've found Sherlock Holmes reincarnated. Besides they say over-washing is worse than lack of. So do I have copy of the investigation?"

"Charlie, you are interestingly the most annoying, aggravating, poorly dressed..."

"Don't forget, uncouth, disrespectful and unwashed."

"Unfucking washed. ARRG. But despite all that you've got something that tells my instincts to keep you here, besides the fact that I need an Elder and a physiatrist on the premises, mainly to look inside my head and tell me what kind of an idiot I am for talking this job in the first place. Just send me the reports and keep the hell out of my way. But," he stared hard at Charlie and talked slow and low. "Don't fuck me around, or you'll regret it."

Charlie leaned on his cane. "This is a two way street. You've my word and ..." He waited as James leaned over his glasses.

"You've mine as well," James replied.

"Deal. Now I need to be left alone for a few minutes. Need to get a feel of something just behind everything here. Has someone taken pictures of all these scribbles?"

"No. But I'll get a set taken before they're washed off and painted over."

"Good. May or may not be possible evidence." Charlie walked around the cell slowly. "Could be good to see if anyone could decipher these. It looks structured and there's regular symbols that repeat themselves." He pointed to the same symbol in three locations on the wall. "If I was to guess I'd say he's writing some kind of ancient language here."

"You think he had anything to do with the killing?"

"Not sure." Charlie ran his hand over a section. "But there's an undercurrent here of something. Not sure what right now. Very old."

James walked out. "I'll get pictures taken this afternoon, I'll need this cell for someone tomorrow."

"Now, I need to be left alone." Charlie barely heard him leave as he sat down and crossed his legs. He put his staff in front of him and set his medicine pouch beside himself and inhaled deeply. "Old winds, old memories dwell here." He closed his eyes, "Very old."

He relaxed, slowly falling into a trance. Charlie reached out and touched the walls where there was writing. A tug, something gently pulled at him. Charlie felt himself being quietly pulled down. He just relaxed, letting whatever it was take him wherever it wanted.

The room faded away, lightning stabbed at him.

Further and further the tendrils pushed him into depths of darkness. Tugging him until a gentle thump. He opened his eyes.

* * *

Carol looked up as she entered the women's smoking area, noticing that it was really just a huge wire cage so the prisoners couldn't jump the fence. *Neither can I* she thought worryingly. The women eyed her warily and she remembered why as she glanced down at her newly acquired prison guard uniform. Damn. *Thought after becoming a detective I wouldn't have to wear one of these again.* The heavy Kevlar vest crushed her breasts flat. *Damn Charlie*. She tried to shift the vest to a more comfortable position with a few shrugs and twists of her shoulders. "Hello ladies," she said as she walked up to a group of women smoking away. They looked her up and down. She waited to see which one was the leader of the group.

"Who's the new kitty kitty?" The heaviest one asked, looking her up and down. It was obvious what she wanted to do with her. "Hey fish, did you bring kneepads with you?"

Carol replied, "Just introducing myself."

"Kiss my ass," was the reply, as she turned away showing her rear to Carol. The others in the group all laughed, it was obvious she was the leader and liked to throw her massive weight around.

"I would, but I can see that prison pocket of yours has been kissed and used more than once. I thought just the guys took it up the rear?" Carol spat back. It was obvious she wouldn't get far with this group. But it was too late to back down now.

The woman spun around, her fat face red with anger, but before she could speak, Carol added, "Say anything more and my baton will be added to whatever else's been stuck up your behind." The others stopped their smiles and stared at Carol and at the fat woman. "Now, it would be appreciated if you would tell me your name."

Scowls wrinkled her face, "Krystal, with a K." She inhaled her smoke, the seething roiling across her face. But she knew enough to know not to tangle with one of the guards. Not unless she wanted to spend more time behind bars. "If it wasn't for the fact that I'm out of here in one week, I'd have you on the ground. And before anyone could help you, I'd Molly whop you and smother that smug face with my anus, cunt. But as much as I like this place, I want out." She growled and spun away, walking off.

Carol caught the clenched fists as the rest of the women followed. "Well then, have a great afternoon." Why did she let him convince her to come here? Most women in jails were rude evil witches and this place was no exception. *Shoulda booked that cruise to Alaska. Then I'd have an excuse not to be here.*

She looked around but didn't see any of the four women that were involved in Charlie's sweat lodge murder. They must have been somewhere else, maybe the mess hall. She exited the cage with a feeling of relief but at least she'd let them know she wouldn't take any crap. *Have to watch my back though, if Krystal gets her chance I'll be her bearskin rug and she'd love to do the skinning. Yup, females can be such bitches.*

* * *

Charlie awoke on a beach. Naked.

He sputtered granules of sand from his mouth and slowly sat up. "Don't like this very much."

Cold chill hung on the misty air as he glanced around. He sniffed. "Old, very old." The sky overhead bore a vibrant purple hue. The errant wind that pulled him here moved from him and whistled among the trees behind him. *Most likely alerting the It or the Them that I'm here.* "Most curious, *They* or *It* does not want to be found. No odours, other than damp sand and salt water. No idea of where or when. I don't get it. What could want this kind of secrecy?" He closed his eyes, wishing himself home. "Unless it doesn't want secrecy?"

Opening them he was still there on the beach. "Well, *They* or *It,* doesn't want anyone in or out. Okay now to get back, because whatever this is, doesn't want anyone returning as well, I can see that. Old trap, old ways. That's the clue."

Something ancient resides here. Very ancient. So before Them or It or Elvis are alerted or shows up, I better leave. Only one way home.

He sniffed the air. *Yes, very ancient and it senses I'm here. Time to go.* Grabbing a rock he smashed it against his head and fell over unconscious. Minutes later Charlie pulled himself up from the cold floor of the cell. Blood trickled down his forehead. He pulled a hanky from his pocket and dabbed at his head as he gathered himself up and tried standing. The cell spun away for a moment, he waited a few moments. "Oh, that's going to leave a nasty welt." He moaned and grabbed his button festooned cap and cane. But I'll be better prepared next time and you my secret friend are no longer a secret. Only who or what are you hiding? And the bigger question why here? So the mystery deepens as old Agi Christie would say. Really got to read some of her crime novels”.

He clanked the cell door closed. “And how does that apply to this murder? I think I need to contact an old friend and see if he can help with this.”

* * *

“John Denton, Curator of UBC Museum of Anthropology speaking. How may I help you?”

“Charlie Stillwaters here. I got your name from Detective Carol Ainsworth,” Charlie said from the phone in the front office.

“Charlie Stillwaters… that name is oddly familiar. Oh, are you the man in the picture that Carol was looking for involving the mayor’s murder last year? Ah, look, I didn’t give her any information other than finding your name.”

“Wow, calm down, John.” Carol was right he was very anal and uptight. “Relax, I’m not looking for you per se. I’m needing some information and I believe you might be able to help me.” Charlie heard him breathe a big sigh of relief. He sounded too uptight, like his Cheerios box had Corn Flakes inside after he opened it or something. “Carol and I are working on a case up here in Prince Rupert.”

“Together? On a case? My, the world changes quickly.”

“Yeah. Let’s say she saw the light. I’ll get right to the point. Now, an inmate has been drawing symbols on his cell walls. Only there seems to be a regular pattern, repeating designs. I get the hunch that he’s writing in a language I don’t recognize and thought you might be the person to decipher it or at least give me an idea if I’m right.”

"Is this for you or Carol? I'm all for helping the law enforcement officials."

"Yes, sorry. Carol. She told me to contact you, rather busy with some tough women in the other side of the pen. She's gotta crack a big case."

"Okay, what have you got? Can you send me pictures via email?"

Email? Man I haven't even been working on the first four letters of the alphabet yet. Charlie looked at the guard on duty and put his hand over the phone. "What's email? Is that short hand for mail delivered by eagles?"

"No, it's electronic mail sent via computers." The guard snickered.

"Can you send these pictures to him via eagle electronic mail? I'll bet that's quicker than snail mail. Eagles tend to have big wingspan. Snails, well, they just leave a trail of slime."

"It's just called email. I can. What's his address?"

"Here, talk to my secretary, he'll do that." Charlie handed the phone over to the guard. The man talked with John for a few moments.

"Done. They'll come back via Ken's email address, which is on your computer. And if you call me a secretary again, I'll plaster that smug smile all over the back of your head." He grunted as he handed the phone back to the native.

"Thanks," Charlie told John on the phone, and the man at the desk, as he hung up and left. He was going to say something rude back, but thought he'd stirred up enough trouble this week. *Now I just got to figure out how to turn on my 'puter in my office.*

* * *

Called from the old slumber it sniffed the air and stared around. *Nothing here now. But*... He glanced around. *Was*. As it spied a misplaced rock. *And…* He stared closely at the rock that he knew was disturbed, after all he knew the position of every rock on this beach. He'd been here a long time. *Red stain. Blood…* It sniffed deeply. *Human, male. Native. But…*

It sniffed again. *Also shaman. This is most interesting.*

* * *

Charlie sat cross-legged before the lodge. His guardians, which no one else could see, patrolled as he closed his eyes. Whatever was out there, he had to check it out. Maybe it was involved with the murder, or at least knew something somehow. He sensed it out beyond the edge of the forest, watching him.

Charlie pulled himself below the earth and floated along until he pulled himself up via a large twin-branched cedar. A portal tree. It had been used recently. The shaman edged past the tree and caught the sight of a small fern-headed being staring back and forth, beginning to get impatient at him simply sitting there. Ghyldeptis? Odd, what would Ghyldeptis be doing here? She was a being of the earth and forests. As he stepped forward a multi-coloured fern-layered stag brayed in her direction. She turned and in a blink vanished into a haze of floating spores and fluttering insects. She had her own beings on guard duty. *Well, in any case, she's not the chatting type and quite harmless*. Still, Charlie wondered why she was checking him, or perhaps the sweat lodge, out. Anything related to the murder?

Just then his black bear on duty growled in his ear, already coming to his rescue if he had to deal with the stag. But both had vanished at the same time. *Hey, it's okay my ursine friend. No deer steaks for you to munch on tonight*. It let him know someone was approaching his body whenever he left it to perform tasks like this one. He closed his eyes. *Carol. Crap, need to go back quick before wolfie makes his own lunch.*

* * *

Carol walked up to Charlie as he sat outside the sweat lodge. *Probably doing one of his woo-woo things, where he communicates with Siberian anteaters or some such thing*. She also knew not to get too close, for he kept spirit animals on duty to watch out for him. Not that she actually believed it.

From somewhere a growl broke the air. Charlie opened one eye. "Hello Carol."

"Oh! Hope I wasn't interrupting something important." She shivered as something seemed to brush past her and this musky rank odour broke the air. "What the…"

"That's my good buddy the Sasquatch and you weren't interrupting me on anything, other than relaxing and working on my suntan."

Carol looked up at the overcast sky. "You keep an invisible Sasquatch on duty while you suntan? Isn't that being a little over protective?"

"Nah, he's looking a little pale as well, kept inside my pouch and all. Kinda like taking your dog for a walk. Otherwise he gets restless and pissing off Bigfoot is not recommended if you want to keep all your limbs attached." Carol looked around, freaked out, as always, at the thought that there were things there that only Charlie was able to see.

"Anyway, reason I came looking for you. Two reasons actually. First, I did talk to Sanchez and he confirms cause of death as the blunt force trauma to the temple but he also said that could be an accident or murder.

However he also thinks that, from the severity of the injury, it was more than likely that Ken was either killed instantly or at least incapacitated immediately by the blow so it is still highly unlikely that Ken would have ended up where he did if he had fallen and hit his head as the rocks were too far away. It's far more likely that he was hit on his head by a rock very similar to those from the fire."

"It's odd though, no one reported their hands being burnt. The rocks are rather hot you know."

"Really Charlie? You surprise me. Yeah, I thought that. I checked with medical but no one had reported a burnt hand after the incident, so I'm guessing either they had some sort of protection, a thick glove or perhaps the sleeve of their uniform, or kicked a rock aside earlier to let it cool down. Trouble is, I can't see us finding the actual rock, so although we seem to know how Ken died, we still don't know who and it's unlikely we ever will." Carol turned to go.

"Hey. You said two things. That's only one thing. What's the other thing?"

"Oh, yeah. I think I might have a problem. Something strange happened to me again."

"Hanging out with me how strange can it get?"

"I had this bizarre man bump into me in Prince Rupert. I met him earlier before on Haida Gwaii in a bookstore. He didn't seem to remember me, but when I mentioned your name he called you Stinkwaters and spat on the ground."

"Hmmm."

"A relative maybe? Cousin?"

"No." Charlie thought for a moment. "Couldn't be, could it? Did he talk slow? Dark hair."

"Jet black with a large, almost hawkish nose."

"Damn. I, ah, don't know him. But if you bump into him again, uh – caution. He's not to be trusted and don't follow him anywhere."

"Hey, if he's not to be trusted you must know him?"

"No, the less I tell you the better. In some of our histories the more a name or a person is mentioned the more they are able to traverse to our realm from another state and that could be what he's trying to do."

"Is this like that Potter thing, the he-who-must-not-be-named dude?"

"Yeah, exactly like that. Trust me on this. Thought I'd be done with him. Trapped him in a cedar."

"Similar to the Lure we battled in Vancouver."

"Yup."

Carol shuddered. How nearly that vile creature had taken over her body on their last adventure in Stanley Park. "So safe to say this he-who-must-not-be-named dude that you supposedly don't know is dangerous?"

"Worse than dangerous. Compare him to somewhere between Attila the Hun and Mary Poppins in PMS mode. Only he's a little more neutral, not really evil, just misguided and very powerful. He also has this empty spot in his guts that never seems to get filled, so never take him to an all-you-can eat diner. You'll be sorry. Now, enough said, more talk about he-who-must-not-be-named dude would trigger more response to his being here."

"Wow, you lead a bizarre life. Just how many strange and powerful beings have you run into in your life?"

"Oh a few, enough to say I'll have my own cheerleading squad at my funeral."

"Charlie I don't even want to know what goes on in your head or what you've done. How do you manage to stay even somewhat sane?"

"TV helps and chewing some of that licorice root fern. Know what Carol, talking to you is one of the best things that has happened to me, keeps me sane and grounded. Makes me feel somewhat like a normal human being."

"Ah thanks Charlie that's the nicest thing you've ever said." *And I doubt he'd ever be a normal human being. I think most pychiatrists would lock him up and melt the key. Unless he confounded them so much they'd end up quitting their day jobs or slashing their wrists.*

"Oh, that wasn't really a compliment more a criticism."

"What? You really are a whack job, aren't you." Carol raised her voice. She never knew what to expect or what would come out of his mouth.

"Thanks for the compliment." He smiled.

"GRRR." She walked back to the prison.

* * *

Charlie limped back to his office where a message waited on his phone. He called the UBC.

"Anthropology, Denton speaking."

"Charlie Stillwaters here. You called, I presume regarding the matter we talked about earlier today."

"Yes. So you're saying an inmate scribbled these all over his cell walls? This is most unusual Mr. Stillwaters as these writings resemble some very old language. I mean very old."

Charlie blinked. How could Bryan have known this? What was in that man's head? "How old, are we talking? Older than Moses stuff?"

"Yes, I'm not sure but many of these inscriptions resemble the writings of Mohenjo Daro and Easter Island, which have most scholars puzzled as to how that is possible. Predates Sanskrit. So whatever he read or saw in a book lately, he probably scribbled over the cell walls."

"Gotta stop you on that one. Our man is in solitary confinement. He is also mentally unstable and hasn't been anywhere near a book or TV, as far as I know, in months and I doubt he's got more than a basic junior high grade. So that's the problem, it looks like something touched him, only what?"

"Touched by what? I don't understand, how he can be writing a five thousand year old language on cell walls?"

"Five thousand? Yikes, that's old. Yeah, I agree, even his grandpa was an old man when the last fluent speaker croaked. Can I ask for a favour? Can you attempt to decipher what he's writing?"

"I'm leaving on holidays, but I'll take it along, might make for some interesting night time excitement."

"You can reach me via this phone number or leave a message at the main phone."

"How about that email address?"

"Email, sure, as well, but I'm not at my desk often. Best to a leave a message at the main desk. Thanks Prof, anyways, for the information. I appreciate it." Charlie hung up and trundled down the corridor towards the library. *Exciting night time entertainment, man he probably gets wet over staring at the newest National Geographic centrefold. Well it takes all kinds. I can only imagine his home life is as exciting, probably sweats over a wild scrabble game and discovering a new herbal tea. No, no don't think he'd be into anything as kinky as herbal, more like an Earl Grey kind of guy. But then many people would think I'm a little off the banana. Especially the monkeys in the zoo.*

I need to study something and need one of those things that hold a lot of information bigger than a book, 'cause I doubt that I'll find any information on ancient languages in this library. I need one of them 'puters Carol tells me about, so I can, how did she say it? Poodle it. Oh and how to operate one could be good knowledge these days, maybe I'll ask the librarian, can't be that hard. Most poodles are quite docile. Dobermans are another matter entirely.

* * *

Carol inhaled deeply at the back of the women's section of the pen as she dragged on her cigarette, since smoking on the grounds, except in the area the convicts hung out in, wasn't allowed. *Meeting that freaky guy was more than unsettling. I'm beginning to think hanging out with this shaman might not be too wise. Not to mention getting involved with out-of-this-world woo-woo dudes. I'm a detective, not a mystic hunter.*

Just then something, a branch, snapped. Carol spun around grasping at her truncheon. A deer scampered away into the woods. *Crap, I gotta relax, way too tense here.*

She returned to finishing her smoke. Carol rubbed the back of her neck. *Still I get the weird feeling I'm being watched or am I just being cynical after meeting that guy.*

From the edge of the clearing a small fern-headed figure watched Carol quietly walk away after she butted out her cigarette.

* * *

"Okay I'll start this one up. Ah, ever use one?" the older man said as he stared at Charlie like he'd just escaped a derelict building.

"Nope. I was told to try oogling the information. Does that mean I stare really hard and the answer magically appears?" He opened his eyes wide.

The older man stared blankly at him, before smirking and readjusting his thick glasses. "Okay. It's called Google. Everything you ever need to know can be searched and found via Google."

Charlie sat down opened his eyes wide and banged his cane on the side of the screen. "Nope, blank. Didn't seem to understand what I was asking it."

The clerk scratched his head. "You need to type it into the keyboard. You do know how to type don't you?"

Charlie raised his ball cap a moment. "Do these look like typing fingers?"

He held them up, all crooked.

He laughed. "No, I suppose not. You'll just have to use two-fingered typing. Now move over and let me get you started. As I said, the main search engine these days is Google. It's taken over from Bing and Yahoo as your main internet search engine."

"Internet? Is this some kind of new fishing gear? I didn't think Mr. Crosby was very good at 'puters, thought that was a might before his time in the fifties. So if Google is a little like oogling things then must you holler Yahoo when you find the thing you're after and scream out Bing-o? I reckon Google took over because it was a lot quieter to use in libraries."

The librarian closed his eyes and shook his head. "It's not named after Bing Crosby. Okay Charlie, now I've pulled up Google. Type in what you're searching for." Charlie did, slowly hitting singular key after singular key. After a couple of minutes they both stared at the screen. "Doesn't look very intelligent to me."

The librarian leaned over and punched enter. "This is like telling it to seek and find, which some days I wished I was doing. Finding a better job." About half a second later a list appeared.

"Ten thousand results in less than a second. Ho, that was quick, this is a smart bugger." He stared at the little cord coming out of the screen. "All that through that little cord?"

"Yup, modern technology. Although we haven't gone wireless yet, which is even better."

"Some new kind of Ouija board that is. Now what?"

"Now take that mouse."

Charlie glanced down at the floor. "What mouse? Don't you guys clean around here? Attracts rodents you know."

The man laughed again. "Okay I can see a quick crash course in computer use is needed. So I'll give you my ten minute crash course."

"Does this require a helmet?"

"I think the ball cap will suffice. Although I can see a baseball bat could be useful right about now as well." His ten minutes turned into two nerve-wracking hours as he showed Charlie how to search, browse and in general look for information on the computer.

Charlie stood up and armed himself with several pages of print outs. "Thanks." He said as he left. "I've done a favour and rewarded your computer with its favourite cheese. Should make it very happy, but I don't think didn't it did the keyboard any good. The mouse looked rather happier."

The librarian put his head in his hands. "And I gave up drinking and smoking for this job."

Chapter Five

Charlie poured over the printouts scattered over his desk, comparing them to the photographs taped to his wall. *So Denton is correct. I see several characters are indeed the same. So what is it he's trying to say and how is he getting something older than Sanskrit in his head?*

Unless something this old has got in contact with him but why is it trying to speak? What could be this ancient in these parts?

He thought a moment. *Is it possible?* He stared at the figures from the prints made on the stone jail walls and ran his fingers over the figure of the outstretched bird.

The inscription from a rongorongo board translation said, "All the birds copulated with the fish. There issued forth the sun." Charlie pursed his lips. "*Oh I don't like where this is going. Birds and fish creatures. I need to visit my old friend stubby fingers and ask a few questions. Who better to ask than the fishy creatures themselves? But first a visit to Bryan and see if I can get some answers out of him.*

* * *

Carol stood outside at the back of the women's section. She'd walked a small distance away from the grounds before deciding it was a good place for a smoke. Even in the pen it was hard to find a place just to be alone. She knew jails were a whole other world, one where inmates were trying to catch you on 'watch your back and your mouth' at all times. She didn't want anyone inside to even know she smoked.

Carol lit her cigarette, inhaled deeply and casually looked around the heavy bushes that had grown in since the woods had been cleared many years ago. In the brush of one section was a small clearing, like deer had been using that as a trail. She spied the ground walking closer. The grass was beaten down, something had regularly been using this area as a trail and recently. She sipped at the coffee-to-go cup in her hand. Not a patch on the HaidaBucks she had on the 'Gwaii' as she called Haida Gwaii just across the bay. Charlie! How did he talk her into this? Some holiday. Oh well, she was getting rather bored laying on the beach. One can only watch the first 38,000 waves crash with enthusiasm. A flutter on a branch in the stillness caught her attention as a chill ran through her.

Just ahead in the bushes, very still, she spotted what appeared to be a dark crouching figure. Carol took another drag exhaling, very slow, casually staring from the corner of her eye. An illusion of the light? Was she sure there was something there?

Glancing out of the corner of her vision, she caught what appeared to be a shadowy figure with slitted eyes staring at her, unblinking. The shiver told her yes, she wasn't alone. Whatever it was never wavered as she looked away, keeping it in the corner of her eye. *Great, I've a demigod stalking me and now some woodland creature checking me out. Why couldn't I just meet some hunky jail guard or forest ranger?*

She stamped out her smoke and casually reached back to unclick her holster and slowly turned to saunter away. Doing a quick double take she made straight for whatever it was, hand on gun. Almost upon it whatever it was blinked, perhaps in shock, and a flutter of branches, a sigh and what appeared to be a green mist like an exploding nearly invisible dandelion, clouded the area for a brief second. *Nothing here?*

Carol lifted the branches and touched the cool ground in one area and then where she spotted the crouching apparition. *Still warm. Vanished like it wasn't even there.*

She scanned the bushes and the ground for some sign of whatever had been there. There on a flat rock lay two tiny figures made of twisted sticks and moss twined together. Carol lifted the tiny stick figures. "How odd."

The slightly smaller figure seemed more rounded, softer. The taller one had one arm much longer than the other. As she peered closer she saw that the longer arm was actually two pieces. *Like a cane?*

Carol looked about. How was this possible? Her and Charlie? How on earth did whatever it was know this? Intelligent enough to conceptualize this and make it. Which meant something else. If that was the case it had been watching them to know. Possibly when they were at the Sweat lodge as well? Didn't Charlie mention he thought he'd been watched?

"Okay not rabid wild dogs then? Something more along Charlie's realm of knowledge and expertise." She uttered as she glanced around before tucking them into her pocket and took another long sip from her cooling coffee. *Oh, I was so hoping being here with him was just going to be a normal type of investigation. Who was I kidding?*

* * *

As the cell door was locked behind him Charlie caught the lyrics of a song from the prisoner's CD player.

And the chains they crash like thunder.
When the lightning strikes
and Zip gun Johnny lies in a pile of his blood,
when the lightning strikes.

A song by Aerosmith?

The prisoner sat there, eyes growing dark. "Snakes dance like frying wires. Screams a shrill, dangle so easy." He spoke.

Charlie cringed. "What was that about? And I don't think it's because he ate some bad pizza."

"Okay so this isn't going to be getting more than a bit strange. So nice day, Bryan, How's it going, eh? Could use a few decorations on the wall." He stared at the jumble of words scrawled on the walls. "Yup, not the openly talkative type. I get that. But get a chalk in your hands and look out he's writing the next War and Peace."

He walked over to the walls to study the writings as Bryan sat muttering and rocking himself. "Go away. Too many here. Too many."

He banged his head several times.

"You're gonna get a one hell of a headache like that. Wonder how many aspirins a day you take."

The big man rose and approached Charlie. "Get out, hurt you. Leave me alone."

"Okay, now I'm getting somewhere. You can talk." He whistled into his pouch as the large native strode up to him. The guard outside unlocked the door, ready to enter. "No, stay out. I've got this under control."

"He's busted up everyone that ever entered his cell." The guard said as he pulled his billy club free.

"Give me a moment first."

"It's your death." The guard waited with his hand on the latch.

The big man took a swing at his head. Charlie quickly ducked and jammed his cane between his would-be attacker's legs. The native fell forward into a heap. Charlie whistled again and mist flooded from his medicine pouch. The man's eyes opened wide.

"You know who this one and his companion are, don't you?"

The guard looked on through the open hatch in the door, bemused.

"What are you talking about, I don't see a thing. Other than some smoke coming from your pocket. That better not be marijuana?"

The big man stared at the two apparitions of a grizzly bear and a large grey wolf as they emerged from the mists. They sat on haunches. Fear rang in his eyes. "So we make a deal. You no touch me and my friends no eat you. Understand? Oh and if you think you can get past those two, I'm packing even bigger hardware." He snapped his fingers and they vanished leaving behind a large growling Sasquatch towering over the shaman. It quickly faded away into the background. Charlie approached the fallen man. "Now let me help you up." He held out his hand.

"I wouldn't do that. No one touches him. He usually freaks," the guard warned.

"Stand down, I've got it under control." He snapped his fingers again and the two guardians reappeared behind him. Bryan stared at them and at his offered hand. "Truce."

The man nodded back and calmly took Charlie's hand. He helped him up. Turning to the guard he said, "Now my friend here is finding this a little uncomfortable with you gawking. You can leave. I'll call when we're done."

The guard put his club back into its holster. "I'll be down the hall. But if he wigs out again, this is your call."

"It'll be okay, I just made him realize it's not worth the effort to take me on."

The guard wandered a few yards down the hall.

"Now my new friend, tell me about yourself. Cause I get that you can talk a lot." He waved at the walls. "Some pretty intense conversations with concrete walls, try people next."

The man began to mutter as he walked back to his solitary bed and began to slowly rock himself, losing interest in Charlie.

“So this begs me to ask the question, why, the day before the murder, did you start writing like this. Records don’t show this before. Up until then you were just a regular certifiable nut. So what changed inside to make you start writing in these characters, which is beginning to look more and more like a language? Only what one and how could you even know this exists? Unless… has some old ancestor resurfaced?” He stared at the man scratching at his face as he rocked.

“Even when I sit in the middle of the forest nothing moves and all is silent. The missing, I know sings to me.” He muttered to himself.

“Well that’s either a cryptic clue or you’re just nuts. Okay, so Mumbles, I was hoping there was some way of reaching you inside there, if there is, you need to give me a sign.” He sat quiet a moment as the man simply rocked back and forth muttering away. “Well, seeing as how I think you’ve left this conversation and this room I might as well be off myself. Nice chat, maybe we’ll do it again over biscuits and tea.”

“Fog, eight.” Bryan spoke clearly.

“Fog, no there was just three in the fog of my guardian spirits.”

“Fog, heavy. Eight.”

“Yeah okay got it. Checked into the loco hotel. I think it’s time to go.”

The man pounded his head. “Fog. Eight.”

“There were some that were just crazy. Too lost in their heads to help.” Charlie felt sorry for the man, wondering what calamity got him into this state.

* * *

Another came here, there are more. I smell the rocks. He is like the shaman of earlier. A mystic of his people. I remember, once my people. The ones that created me. I try to reach out again. The skies darken and I sleep on the rocks. My rocks.

* * *

Charlie sat across from a Florence Sanderson. She looked serene, older, probably had ten years on him. Hair greying, laugh lines adorned her face, signs of aging, fat deposits around her eyes and cheeks. His niece and her kids sat in the booth across from them. He'd agreed to look after Sandy's two kids on Sundays for the summer in order to help her out. She'd agreed to buy him dinner in return.

"Now, I'm a bit confused. Your maiden name is Henderson. My records show that when you got married you already had Thomas. But you were married under Sanderson and there were no Hendersons at St. Mary's Residential School, but three Thomas Johnsons." He flipped through the old folder he'd been handed earlier in the week. "They state that you gave him up for adoption under the residential program. Only the two that died don't match your son's birthdate, no matter what name he was registered under."

"No, I never did. When they were taking kids into the residential program I was getting remarried at the same time. I don't know what happened." She looked perplexed.

"From what I'm seeing I think there's a remote possibility that out of the three kids admitted that year, all under the name of Thomas Johnson, your son could be still alive. Two died, one was listed as given up for adoption."

"I was told at the time that he had died but I'd already gone up to live with my new husband in the Territories, that's why my name changed, which didn't work out and I moved back here last year to look after my dying mother."

"Yellowknife?"

"Correct."

"And you never questioned it."

"Never saw the body, nor could afford to attend the funeral. But I remember him being a big boy, big baby. I think he was barely two when they came for him. You gotta remember also that back then you didn't question the government, what they said…"

"…was the correct and right thing."

"Yes, I was already up north when he died. But if you need proof he's my son, I remember him having a mole on his left arm, just below his elbow, here." Florence pointed to the inside of her elbow. A honk outside. "My ride just pulled up. It's a mole, jagged, kind of star shaped, from what I remember. Call me whether you think it's him or not. If it is, I really miss him."

As she got up to leave, Charlie pushed all his papers back into his folder. "I'll join you after I escort her out and visit the restrooms." Charlie said to Sandy as he got up.

Charlie said goodbye to Florence and walked over to the washrooms. He stood waiting, pacing while the men's restroom was occupied as another man approached and stood behind him.

Charlie stared at him, "They're both occupied."

"Well, I can wait, but not for long. I'm George and judging by your ball cap looks like you're a baseball fan?" He wiggled slightly side to side, obviously needing to go far worse than he mentioned.

"I'm Charlie, and yes, I've a cabin up on Haida Gwaii and other than TV there isn't much else to do. Got hooked on watching the Expos many years ago."

"You still support them? Even though they're gone?"

"Hey, once a fan always a fan. My girlfriend Lucy got me hooked on baseball. The first time I went to her place there was a game on. Kinda got attached to them, and her."

"Ah, first love. And the rest, as they say, is history. As for myself I'm a New York Mets fan."

"Oh, and I was beginning to like you." They both laughed as the stall door to the men's opened.

He returned to the table with Sandy Two-Moccasins and her two youngsters. The girl was scribbling wildly in her colouring book as Charlie sat down. "What are you drawing?" Charlie asked, hoping what he was doing here with Florence was right. He didn't want to hurt either of them, Florence and especially Griz. The man would probably go ballistic. *What if I got the hopes up for these two? God...*

"God." He thought as Cindy yelled it out.

"God?" Sandy sputtered, "nobody knows what God looks like."

"In a moment they will." She kept scribbling away until she showed everyone a glob of red and green scribbles.

Charlie smiled. "I'd say that's probably an accurate description. But I think you missed some orange over here."

Sandy looked up from her paper, hardly glancing at her daughter's drawing. "Sorry, had to finish this article. The papers say another wave of red tide is sweeping across the North Shore, looks like we can't go clamming again this summer."

"Wouldn't happen if Thunderbird were here, one of his jobs was keeping the waters clean for his people and the salmon." Her uncle Charlie spoke from under his well-worn, button-festooned Montreal Expos

Baseball cap.

"Thunderbird, Raven. You keep talking on about these fairy tale creatures as if they're real. The red tide is just from the white man polluting our waters and overfishing our fish. Hey, didn't I say to settle down?" she bellowed again.

The two kids continued pushing and tormenting each other, nearly upending a waitress with arms full of plates, as one tore off up the aisle.

"She pushed me."

"He pushed me first."

Charlie frowned, "nothing to do with the white man, he doesn't understand native spirit. It has to do with Thunderbird not being here. His job was to keep the waters clean and pure, keep the salmon safe from the Water-Spirits and the Orcas."

His niece glared back. "Not sure who's more whacked-out, you and your crazy ideas or the white-eyes who think they know better."

Charlie simply smiled back. "You pay the lady and let me talk to these two misbehaving youngsters. They remind me of an old tale about no doing good."

He rounded up the kids roaming in the aisle. "Come outside and let me tell you what happened to a young thunderbird who didn't listen to his parents."

"Whoopee! A story!" They followed happily. Unlike their mother, they both loved the old tales their great uncle told them, especially as they were always accompanied by chocolate treats.

The waitress picked up the paper as they rose. Charlie caught the lower half of the front page as she began to clean up.

Cessna goes down in heavy fog and sudden thunderstorm yesterday. Eight aboard.

"Wait a second kids. Can I see that?" He glanced at the brief story. *Private chartered Cessna went down this morning in heavy fog. Bound for Sandspit Airport. Suspected eight aboard. No signs of wreckage as search begins along planned route.*

"Oh, I think our friend in the jail isn't as crazy as we think."

"What friend in jail?" Sandy asked nodding for the bill, knowing the two kids were beginning to annoy the rest of the patrons in the restaurant and wanting to herd them outside.

"Come on Uncle Charlie." They wailed together. Charlie reached into his pocket and threw two loonies on the table. "I'll buy it. Look, I'll tell you youngsters the story next weekend. I've got to get back to the jail; this is very important."

Both kids put on big sulking frowns.

"What, go now? You can't buy that paper it's the restaurant's copy." Sandy spat, "You promised these two a story."

"Sorry, buy the restaurant another one then."

"But they're free."

"Oh, in that case I'll take it." He grabbed back his coins kissed the two youngsters on top of their heads, deftly slipped a few wrapped chocolates into their pockets. "You too behave, the candies will keep you wired up for now and I'll tell you the story next week. Sorry, gotta go. My intuition is rarely wrong and I think lives depend on this." Much to the chagrin of their mother he tucked the newspaper under his arm, grabbed his cane and limped down the aisle.

"Incorrigibly rude that man sometimes and worse I let my kids out on the loose with him." She muttered to the waitress. "But I've got no one else that can watch them during summer holidays on Sundays. Oh, and I'll pay for the paper as well." She watched Charlie hailing the taxicab as he glared at the headlines.

Cindy and Tyler were already unwrapping their chocolates and quietly stuffing their faces.

"Actually, I'm surprised he can read."

* * *

The next morning Charlie entered Bryan's cell again. He sat there rocking, mumbling away. "So, I know you know somewhere inside you can hear me, but I suspect your head is full of visions. No wonder you're nuts, I would be too if I could see what you can." The man rocked, ignoring the shaman as he spoke. His eyes were cloudy, as usual. "If you can, cut the mumbling crap. I know there's a man inside there and I know why others think you are crazy, but you're not and I'm beginning to think I may know what is wrong."

"So much, so much inside." He rocked back and forth. "Hard to think."

Charlie could see he'd scratched his arms raw.

His eyes grew dark, black.

"Betrayal's knots. Time's unravelling. Hunger's taste and snakes frying."

"You mentioned snakes frying before. What does that mean?" He stared from some black pit inside and blinked twice. Charlie reached over to stop Bryan from scratching himself again.

"What are you gay or something Shaman? Touching me like that?"

"No, trying to stop you from scratching yourself." He let go.

He looked down at his scabbed and bleeding arms. "Who did this?"

He began to scratch himself as he looked at Charlie.

"Why, you, and you're doing it now." Charlie blurted, unsure what was happening. Split personality? Or just psychotic madness?

The man looked up and as he did his hand fell away. Skin bleeding from under his fingernails. "At what," He glanced down again, "You did this?" He began to scratch again. "That's obvious."

"It's obvious you're missing a few screws and a couple of washers." He muttered to himself. "But I don't know how yet. But if there's a way I'll get you better."

He sat down next to the man as he mumbled away. "Look, I can help you, but you need to step up to the plate and help me." He pulled the paper from his back pocket and held the headlines before the man's face. "That plane is missing. You know it. I know you know it."

"Fog, eight." He blurted staring straight ahead, as if he was seeing something in his mind.

"Yes. The headlines read 'eight missing in plane that went down in heavy fog'. Okay, so we're in agreement. Now it's still missing. Must have gone off course. I need to know where it is and is anyone alive. I've read your file and know you never reconnected with your parents after residential school. You prove to me you're for real and there's someone left inside there and I'll find your parents and see if I can help with these visions."

He sat quietly as the man swung his head back and forth quickly as if speed reading the paper over and over again, mumbling away. He grabbed the paper quickly and shredded it before falling into his bed. "Help, help. Need help."

Charlie got up and signaled the guard. As he turned to leave a hand touched his shoulder. "Damn," he jumped. "I usually sneak up on others unannounced."

Bryan's eyes cleared for a moment. "CE348571." He closed his eyes.

"CE348571, what does that mean?"

"Fog, eight."

"Okay," he cautioned the guard to hold off a second. "The Cessna that went down, do you know where it is and is anyone alive? Help save their lives and I'll know that there's someone inside that I can help."

Bryan hit his head as the mists began to return to his eyes. He stumbled back to his bed. "So much inside. Two. Forest, heavy." He howled in pain. "Hurt, pain."

Charlie rubbed his hands together vigorously and placed both his hands on the man's head. Concentrating he willed as much calming energy as he could to flood into the man's head. Heat flooded the shaman. Charlie fought to keep whatever it was from entering him. "Oh, man, is there a lot of shit inside you and whatever it is wants me as well. Now, I can't keep this up long. Do you know where the plane is?"

"Mother."

Charlie thought a moment, concentrating on keeping whatever was in this man from spreading to him. "There is no island named mother."

"Mother, need see. Keep out, head." He pulled away and pounded his head. "Quick, One time. Map." He quietly curled into a ball and began to keen like a rabbit did in pain. Charlie grabbed him and slapped his face twice. "No, don't lose me. I'll find your mother. But you must help me find these people. Guard, cuff him and call the warden. Now. I haven't much time."

The guard radioed the warden.

"He's on his way down, but he wants to talk to you."

Charlie grabbed the walkie talkie.

"What the hell is this?" the warden blurted out.

"I won't explain now, but I haven't much time. This man knows where the Cessna that went down yesterday is. But I'm losing him. You're going to have to trust me on this."

"Okay, but he makes a break for it. My orders are to shoot first." The warden's voice echoed back.

"Okay, tell the warden to meet me in the main lobby where the large map of BC is." Charlie and the two guards ushered out the howling Bryan after they cuffed him. "When we're done I've got some herbal potion that if I'm right might help get rid or reduce what's happening to you. Now hurry along."

Chapter Six

He begins to get too close. I must let the master know. He will not like this. I turned from the hallway as they ushered the yammering native down the hall. The shaman is beginning to be a real problem.

* * *

They assembled in the front lobby where the large nautical map of the Northern BC coast sat on the wall. "Lock down the front doors. What the hell is going on with this crazy man and why bring him here?" The warden growled as they cleared the room.

"I need him un-cuffed now. I can't keep his consciousness present for much longer, I'm losing him to the madness raging inside." The two guards stared at Charlie, the keening Bryan and their boss. Charlie rubbed his hands together and held them to the crying man's head.

He breathed deep. "Fuck. I haven't got time for this. Okay, one suspect move and I'll shoot him and you as well. Go ahead."

They did and Charlie pulled him closer to the map and whispered into his ear. The mumbling man began to run his hands over the map haphazardly as Charlie held one hand at the side of his head. Intense concentration evident on the shaman's face as he struggled to keep Bryan's consciousness in control.

"What is that crazy bastard doing?" One of the guards uttered.

"He's seeing; he sees with his hands." Charlie glared at the warden. "You won't believe me, but that's why he wrote all over the walls. To see something."

"He's what? Okay enough, take him back to his cell and lock him back up. Should probably lock you up with him for the night as well. I don't know which is more nuts, Bryan, or me for listening to you."

The guards moved forward.

"Now, Bryan I need to know now." The native man rolled his eyes skyward and pointed to a spot. "Fog, eight. CE348571. Two, hurry."

He pointed to Banks Island on the map. "It's a big island. Is that for sure?"

Bryan jammed his finger into the lower left half of the island. "Fog eight. CE348571. Here, right here. Two left." The guards pulled his hands behind his back and snapped the cuffs back on. As they hauled him down the corridor he continued to mutter away in gibberish, foam dribbling from his mouth, completely lost now to whatever was possessing him inside.

Charlie grabbed the warden's pen from his suit pocket. "Do I make the call or have we gone through all of this for nothing?"

"You trying to tell me he knows where the Cessna went down from yesterday? That's not only absurd, but that flight was bound from Prince Rupert to Haida Gwaii. Banks is way off course."

"Tell me this. If he's locked up in confinement, how could he have heard or possibly have even known about this incident?" Charlie asked. "The man read to me word for word the headlines from yesterday's paper." He lied, but it was time for desperate measures.

"Okay, I'll humour you." He pulled his cell phone and called the RCMP office. Charlie stared at the map as he talked slow and then rapidly to the person on the other end. "Don't forget to ask what CE438571 means."

The warden shook his head as he hung up the phone. He stared at

Charlie. "It's the serial number on the wing of an airplane. That plane. How the fuck did he know that? They haven't searched there yet, because it's quite a way off the intended flightpath. How is it even possible that he knows any of this?"

"If they find the plane, let me know. I'll be in my office and I'll explain what I know of him and other shit that will make you doubt everything you ever believed in." Charlie limped heavily leaning on his cane as he left the room. He needed to rest. Trying to keep what was inside of Bryan from entering him took a huge mental drain. "Oh and tell me how many are left alive."

"Charlie, I may have said this to you before, but go to hell." The warden paused as he stared at the map on the wall and circled the spot Bryan pointed to. *Unless of course you're bloody right and then that raises one hell of a lot of questions. A lot of questions I don't want to answer.*

* * *

Carol stood in the clearing. *It's always here, why here? And why do you want to contact me? Something about this clearing then.*

She thought a moment. *I'll bet if I ask the shaman he's going to say you're some kind of spirit of the forest. Shy I think, don't get that you're a threat, can't communicate. Well except for stick creatures. I'm also to assume something very important happened in order for you to try to reach me.* Cedar leaves fluttered to the ground. The bushes all around her waved, going in a circle, around and around. *Stop. I get that you're upset and scared as well. It is also obvious that you can pick up my thoughts.*

Carol closed her eyes and sat in the centre of the clearing. *So I learned something from the crazy shaman. Never trust your damn eyes.*

She relaxed and unfocused her eyes. *Like looking at those hidden three-D images*. There, blending into the bushes. A wavering blur. She struggled even harder to keep her vision unfocused. A face began to emerge from the foliage of a young girl, moss sprouting on her face and from the top of her head like hair. Ferns grew haphazardly down her back and hung off her shoulders. She smiled at Carol as if she knew that Carol could now see her.

Carol got up and slowly began to walk towards the figure in the bushes. In a breath it vanished. "Hmmm, still shy then. Well I've at least got a face to put to this. Let's go talk to Charlie and see if he knows who you are."

* * *

A few hours later Charlie was disturbed from his nap by a knock on the door. The warden entered and closed the door behind him. "I owe you a word of apology. Search and Rescue flew over the area and at the coordinates he marked they've spotted signs of wreckage. We'll know shortly if there's any survivors." He stuck out his hand. "It appears that I'm wrong and that you were right. Now, how did you know what Bryan can do?"

Charlie yawned and stared at his hand. "Ever get those cuticles trimmed?" He reached up and shook the warden's hand. "But, I will say thanks for the honesty. You're beginning to grow on me. I went out into the forest behind the grounds today and found a few herbs. The kitchen is brewing up a potion for Bryan."

James stood there patiently. "Now here's the part I told you about earlier. I think he's what we Haida call, a beholder."

"A what? You Shaman, irritate the crap out of me. But, and this is a big but, as much as it pisses me off to say this, you surprise me and I think I have greatly underestimated you. I also believe you are a man of your word. I don't profess to know how you do what you do, but whatever it is you do, I'm impressed."

"Thanks. Now, you aren't going to like this, but I'm telling you because you asked. A beholder in our past history, would have become a shaman. He sees visions in his head and through his hands can also see the past or visualize whatever he's touching depending on the depths of his powers. Hence he needed to touch the map to be able to see the area, in his head, of where the plane went down."

James shook his head. "This is totally messed up. No one, myself included believes this. Yet he found that plane. All I'm going to tell the media is that one of our inmates, who I won't reveal, professed to have a dream about the plane. If you're questioned, that is all they need to know. Got it? I can't have word getting out about this or the inmates will get all freaked out and possibly his life could be endangered."

"Yeah, that's a pretty accurate description of part of the truth. But, I understand politics and will go along with it. Oh, and I need another favour. I need to know if there's any record of his parents. To the best of my knowledge he never found them out after getting out of the schools."

"I'll get Jenkins to dig into his records and see what we can find."

"And?" Charlie stood there grinning.

"And what?"

"And?" Charlie opened his eyes at the warden.

James pursed his lips. "And again thanks, as much as it behooves me to say it." With that James walked out.

The shaman pulled his cap low over his head and slumped back in his chair. *Okay, now back to my main snooze, as most cats would say.*

* * *

There also was another. He was here. I smell my rocks. He sees others, myself, in his head. He knows. I will talk to him, if possible. Does he live in a place like me, alone?

* * *

Charlie sat down beside the huge man sitting by himself at the table. As usual all the others were full. "Hey Griz, how's it going. I got few extras for you." He put down his heavy plate overloaded with chicken and potatoes. The big man stabbed at the pile and loaded it into his own plate. He wasn't talking much, still brewing in that massive pile of hate and anger inside him.

"Good." He gulped down his food. "If you got bad news I don't want to hear it." Charlie had heard he'd already gotten into two fights this week with others, most likely for no particular reason.

"I actually visited with a Florence Sanderson, we had a chat while I was visiting my niece and looking after her two kids. Apparently, and I checked the records, there were three Thomas Johnsons in St. Mary's at the time of your, shall we call it, incarceration. Two died under circumstances that aren't in the files and they reported to her that one was her son. Seems sloppy paperwork has led her to believe you are dead. I rechecked the birth records and I don't think her son died. I might be staring at him."

Griz swatted both plates across the room. Clanking cutlery resounded. Everyone else stopped eating, several backing up in their chairs. Several guards approached the table as Griz stood up, his fists shaking. "I'll kill them all for putting me in that place."

"Griz sit down now. There's more." The guards approached as Charlie yelled at him. The shaman waved them away as the large man sat back down, the chair groaning under his weight. All this man knew was fighting and retaliation.

Rage and something else, tears, fought in his eyes. "All I want to do, all I've ever wanted to do was see her and ask questions. I was told I was given up for adoption."

Charlie summoned up his courage and reached out to put his hand on the large man's fist, hopefully trying to ground the up-swell inside. "You might get a chance soon. But can I get you to roll up your sleeve on your left arm?"

Griz looked at him menacingly. "What is this about? I don't take needles, not like half the druggies around here."

"No, I need to see something. You're going to have to trust me." Charlie could feel the anger roiling inside the man.

"Here's the only thing I trust." He pulled up his sleeve and flexed his arm.

"Crap those muscles would make the Incredible Hulk jealous and you ain't green."

Charlie peered closer. "But I'm very sorry. You're not her son. She said you have a jagged star shaped mole on your left arm."

"Why didn't you bloody say so." He rolled down his sleeve. Everyone in canteen was quietly watching the two, wondering when all hell was going to explode and one aka shaman would end up splattered all over the floor.

"What you bastards staring at?" He growled as he stood up and rolled slowly down one arm and rolled up the other. It showed that he obviously had nothing better to do than work out in the weight room.

"I bet you can countertop-press more than three of us put together."

"Over four hun and it's bench press," he grumbled. He flexed his exposed bicep on his right arm. All Charlie could see was muscle on top of muscle, on top of more muscle. Griz straightened his arm out. "Is this what you're after?"

There in the crook of his right arm, lay a small jagged mole like star. It was Charlie's turn to let out a deep breath. He had for a few moments thought he'd been so wrong on this one. That his intuition had let him astray and that Griz wouldn't take it well.

There were times to say something funny or sarcastic. This wasn't one of those times. "You're him. I think I've found your mother. I'll try to arrange a meeting in the next couple of weeks." He kept it simple.

Griz opened his mouth and gasped for air, unable to vocalize over the emotions flooding out of him. Tears burst from those angry red eyes as he rolled down his sleeve. For that moment the angry mountain of a human being was gone and only a teary-eyed young boy remained. They sat like that for long moments as Thomas released everything he'd been storing up inside his whole life. Charlie simply held his hand over the man's until his fist collapsed and his open palm rested on the table. "She did say she can't wait to see you."

Griz looked at him, tears so unbecoming to the person spewing them. He didn't sob, just great wracking tears flooded down. "Thanks," was all he gasped, struggling to remain as composed as possible. He knew it might not last long and he didn't want anyone to interfere or make light of him. Not now. It wouldn't go well.

"Guards, take this man to his cell. He needs some alone time."

Two guards slowly took Griz as he wiped at his tears. Charlie pulled one guard aside and whispered. "Don't say anything to him, just let him be alone."

As they walked out Charlie picked up the two plates and headed back to the cooking area to clean them off. Everyone in the room who just witnessed the second coming of Jesus, sat silent. And then like the scene in 'Dead Poets Society', where Robin Williams is applauded by all the students standing on their desks at the end after he's been fired,several began to clap as Charlie quietly limped from the room with his cane.

Chapter Seven

Charlie sat Sandy's pair of misbehaving kids beside him on their patio. The meeting earlier in the day with Florence had gone well. She also had choked over the news that Thomas was indeed her son. "Now, the story I promised you last week. Only I won't tell it if you're acting up."

Cindy poked Tyler in the back. "See, you need to be still."

"And that goes for you as well missy. Now, if you two can sit quietly, I'll give you each half of this chocolate bar and the best behaved one, gets the rest of this one." He broke a third off the second one and crunched it down. Amazingly, the pair sat quietly as Charlie munched on the chocolate bar. "Okay, here's some for you guys." He doled out equal halves. "Where do I begin? Oh yeah, there lived a family of Thunderbirds, once, up on Northern Vancouver Island. They had a very young son who, like you little tykes, didn't behave. He used to transform all the time into a human. He'd tilt his beak back like this and pull back his face and shed his feathers." The old man opened his mouth widely trying to stretch his skin back and pulled at his face making grotesque grimaces.

"Cool," the boy said.

"Gross." His sister frowned.

Charlie shivered and shook himself, all over, showing them how the young creature would wash its feathers away and become a little boy. "His parents warned, 'Do that too many times and you could become trapped in a human shell'. Only the boy wouldn't listen, he enjoyed pulling pranks and every time he remained longer and longer as a human as he enjoyed being among them, making friends. Most Thunderbirds are raised individually."

"Kinda like Raven, the trickster, right Unc?" the boy spoke up.

"Yes, but Raven was born to pull stunts, not Thunderbirds. Their job was to hunt killer whales and ancient Water-Spirits, beings so old no one remembers their names, we used to call them Tsagan Xaaydagaay, the underwater people or today, Wasgo."

"Wasgo, sounds like rascal," the girl muttered.

"No sounds evil, wolves have great awful teeth to crunch their prey with." He made a snapping sound.

"Yes, the Wasgo is often depicted with the tail and head of a wolf. On his head a blowhole like a killer whale and great powerful fins instead of legs. His prey are killer whales."

"Orcas? But they're nice."

"No stupid, they eat seals and fish. That's why they're called killers. Silly."

"Ah you are right. But everything has something that it is afraid of. Usually something hunts something else. Wasgos hunt and eat Killer whales. They are often shown with their tails wrapped around the killer whale before …"

"Before they eat them whole, like this." He gulped loudly.

"Ewww." She squealed.

"Being part wolf they can travel onto land as well, the fins transform to legs with great paws and long claws. The Wasgos would terrorize the Haida villages, eat anything they can find. They have such great appetites. Besides, if no one hunted the Orcas they'd get too many and they'd eat all the salmon. The Water-Spirits loved messing up the water after a great feast. They Love to live in slime and filth, hiding in pools of dirty water. Kinda like your rooms."

The two kids frowned at him, not liking being told off.

"Only the Wasgo have one enemy they fear. The great Thunderbird. One day the Water-Spirits got together with the killer whales and vowed between them to get rid of the Thunderbirds for the Thunderbirds ate the orca as well. "They are too strong for us, they are fearsome hunters. We grow weary of always searching the skies, looking out for them. If we get rid of the young one, who likes to tease the humans, then his parents will become depressed and return to their own lands."

So killer whales and Water-Spirits together transformed themselves into children and began to befriend the young boy, telling him the things they learned from the humans in a place they called school. "Teachings. We learn much from there. The humans are very smart.'"Hearing the wonderful stories of this place called school he decided to join his new friends, relishing the opportunity to play even more tricks.

Only the Water-Spirits and killer whales placed a spell on him, and he couldn't remember that he was really Thunderbird. The white man took him to the Ministry, where discovering he had no parents, at least none that he could speak of, they declared him an orphan and took him far away to one of the residential schools on the mainland. There he stayed for the whole year before being allowed to return. Only he never did return because his parents were right. Stay in that form too long and you become like them and forget who you are and lose your powers.

"He's trapped in human form forever now", it was whispered among our people.

The Water-Spirits and the Orcas were correct, their plan had worked. His parents were heartbroken and left the island, but not until they had discovered the trick played on their son. So the Salmon people disappeared, rumoured to have been taken by the Thunderbirds as a way of torturing the killer whale people and the Water-Spirits.

In grief they transformed themselves into mountains along the coast, dark brooding mountains that always had clouds and thunder gathering around them in sorrow. And that's what will happen to you if you don't listen to your mother. The Water-Spirits have large teeth, bigger than the whale's. Very sharp, and they use the young children to floss between those teeth before swallowing them whole." The old man made a large gulping sound pretending to dangle something in his mouth first.

They stared up at their great uncle with eyes as big as saucers.

"Are you scaring my kids with native stories again?" Sandy said as she walked up to them. "And feeding them chocolate?"

Charlie winked, "Sometimes the old oral stories my granddad told me when I was their age had more than one purpose." He smiled as the two jumped up and clutched at their mother's legs, obviously terrified by his story. It had worked.

"When Thunderbird has returned to his people, go to the river and listen to the waters. You will hear the rush of the salmon people returning, like no sound you ever heard before. But be careful. Watch the skies for him. He'll use the lightning snakes that live under his wings to hunt for Water-Spirits or killer whales to devour, or," he whispered "bad boys or girls to snack on." Charlie bit down hard at them and as he did he slammed his cane against the metal garbage can beside him.

The two hung onto their mother's legs screaming. "Now look what you've done! Scared the crap out of them."

* * *

As Carol approached the sweat lodge Charlie ducked out its entrance; she had thought to find him here. "Hey grabbing a snooze in there or you doing your woo-woo thing?"

"I'm woo-wooing. There's something bugging me, or as you say some critical clue we haven't found."

"What makes you say that? This is most unusual for you."

"Call it intuition. This all began after the first meeting with the same group."

"So are you thinking something happened in the first one? Which begs me to ask the question. Why did you come here, because invariably you always know more than you let on?" Carol prodded him as they stood out back by the sweat lodge.

"To investigate the death of the Elder."

"No, Charlie it's not. I'm not stupid. We've worked together before. There's something else going on here."

He squinted one eye. "Are you interrogating me?"

"If I have to. We need to be on the same page."

"I ain't talking, Copper." He said gruffly and laughed.

"Okay, have it your way." Carol pulled out her baton and tapped it on her other hand. "This can go easy or this can go hard. Have it your way." She laughed back.

"Stop, I give up. Never been a tough one under torture. I got jumped once by a roving band of badgers, tied up."

Carol slid her baton back in her holster. "Here, we go again." She sat quietly, knowing there was another crazy story unfolding here.

"They gave me the famous badger torture test. Consisting of making me watch old westerns, where the Indians always bite the big one. I confessed and they got the contents of my entire winter stash of smoked salmon from my lock up safe. But I managed to turn the tables and knock them out. Quite the epic battle that was." He waved his cane around like he was fending off some vile creatures. "Ended up tying them up and making them watch reruns of Bullwinkle and Rocky cartoon shows. They never came near my place again."

She shook her head, laughing.

"And what I didn't tell you is that I'd won the whole lot in a poker game with three squirrels, a rather amorous raccoon - she was a handful after three glasses of fermented cherries - and an otter very good at sleight-of-hand."

"Hey! You don't have a safe." Carol shook her head.

"That's what I told them. I caved and gave them my social insurance number."

"You don't have one of those either. I remember doing a search through all the Government databases when we met in Vancouver."

"Hadn't, got one now. Needed it for this job. But the badgers didn't know that either. So I gave them the number to the local pizza store. Apparently they have this thing for tomato sauce and basil, gets them high. Old Joe Crow the owner, still to this day, get these annoying calls that he swears is a fax machine gone haywire, only I know it's the badgers twittering away."

"Okay Charlie. Stop. Enough of the deflection. Why are we here? And don't make me use this." She stroked her baton.

"How do I put this? As you know I'm fairly connected to the current, as I call it, Earth news, the spirit guides and any supernatural events as they occur. Well two weeks before my es-steamed preditor…"

"I think you mean esteemed predecessor."

"That's the guy. I got these feelings of a strong disturbance happening. Kind of like a predator to an earthquake."

"Predecessor."

He tapped his cane on the ground. "I managed to discover it happened somewhere in the Prince Rupert area. Then I heard about the Elder being killed."

"By whom? This isn't public knowledge."

"Well let's just say I got a few chipmunks on the inside."

"Definitely got a few nuts loose."

"Hah, funny. I'm trying to be serious."

"Okay sorry. And this disturbance happened around the same time as the original sweat?"

"Yes, so whatever occurred triggered something in the spirit world. My guess is that Ken awoke or got below the surface of one of the people in the sweat."

"And whatever he found he got killed over. I think we need to get back to your office and get into his computer files."

"Yeah, all I managed to do is turn it on."

"I'm surprised you could do even that."

"Me too, although I've had help from nimble fingers George in the library. He gave me few tips."

"Yeah, like don't play with amorous raccoons. Okay let's see what I can do."

"Man, here I've been talking to my nephews and nieces about the oral legends and never for a moment realizing that it could be true."

"Yes, but if this is an oral legend, come to life. It happened a long time ago, hence the term legend. How is he, she or it, to be gender specific, alive. If Thunderbird was transformed into a human, that human would have died long before Christ was born." Carol scratched her head.

"Don't know, but natives believe in a form of reincarnation, in that when you die you can be reborn in the next generation and often the parents will rename their baby based on what they see in its eyes as it is born or shortly thereafter."

"Maybe I can help you with that. I've also had an inmate doing the same thing as one of yours. Writing on the walls. They keep washing it off before I get to see it but I'll try to sneak in tomorrow morning and take some pictures."

"If you do, I'd say send them to me, but I haven't got a phone."

"No, but did you mention you're using the library's computer."

"I'll see what their email address is and send it."

Charlie leaned on his cane and scratched at his baseball cap. "Don't you think it odd that after the first meeting, we've got possibly two people scribbling what looks like an ancient language on their walls, both mumbling gibberish?"

"Which means that something happened in that first meeting and the Elder was silenced because of it." Carol pondered.

"I think my esteemed predilactor stirred up some kind of old memories. Sweats like hypnosis have been known to do that."

"It's bloody predecessor." She shoved her hand into her pocket. "Oh, I nearly forgot the reason I'm here to see you." Carol pulled out the two stick creatures.

"You're into origami? Great job with the cane, but you could have put a miniature smoke in one hand on yours." He smiled.

"Bugger off. Actually origami is done with paper."

"Well, stick is raw paper."

"Grrr, you drive me crazy. No, I found these left behind for me. I go out for a smoke outside of the fences and …"

"You felt like someone is watching you." He finished her sentence.

"Yes. How'd you know?"

"I get the same thing. Felt it a few times out there and every time I try to search mentally for it, whatever it is vanishes."

"I had these left behind one day. I tried the next day to do that crazy unlock your eyeballs and defocus thing you showed me in Vancouver and saw this young lady, ferns growing out of her head. Well actually that could have been her hair and moss adorning her body."

"She is called Gyhldeptis, a Haida legend, name virtually means Lady Hanging Hair. Her hair is usually moss hanging down and she has the ability to read your unguarded thoughts, knows if you're good or not."

"Is she the Haida version of Santa, then?" Carol smirked.

"Ha, ha, ha. You got me back. She is a synthesis of nature and earth. A being of great kindness and gentleness. Can't speak but translates via the wood and earth. Hence the wooden creatures, she's trying to contact you. Although odd that she's reaching out or just perhaps curious about you, yet she seems to be avoiding me."

"Yeah, I'm better looking. But you're right, it would make logical sense for her to contact you. What do you think she would want?"

"That you'll have to find out for yourself. In white terms, she's the native version of Dirk Gently's concept of 'The Fundamental Interconnectedness of All Things' from Douglas Adams."

"The what? Where did you get that? You must read a lot of rubbish."

"Well, what can I say, I live by myself all winter. I've got TV, no Expos, it's the off season and they've been sold to some American joint. Actually I just like certain authors, Douglas Adams is one that has a pretty good handle on things 'out there.'"

"Douglas Adams? I only read police reports and documents related to investigations. Never liked reading, Hey, there's the Blue Jays."

"Yeah, go yammering birds that walk around looking like they're mad or stoned on fermented millet. Even crows can't take those fellas. But there's the library, lots of books to lend out. I like that idea, you whites stole the concept of Potlatching on that one. They've lots of Douglas Adams."

"And I'll bet lots of Agatha Christie."

"Yeah, they've got a shelf or two dedicated to her and some simpleton named Cat in the Hat. Man that guy can barely write."

"Dr. Seuss. That's kids' books."

"In a jail? Oh, and I thought they had a whole section made for midgets and simpletons or newbies to the whole concept of reading or writing."

"Yeah, I imagine there's a few here who can't read and write. What a better way to teach them. Anyway, this Gyhldeptis. You say she's supposed to be completely harmless. What's she got to do with me? Or this case?"

"Don't know yet. Maybe whatever happened here in those sweats she knows something about? Maybe nothing. Except for..."

Carol groaned. "Let me guess. Except for 'The Fundamental Interconnectedness Of All Things'."

"Yeah, FIOAT for short or in my language the efing-oats."

"What?" She worked it out in her head. "You drive me mad."

Charlie thought a moment. "You know the old saying? Country girls and rock and roll never get old."

"Ah let me guess another Roy Orbison classic."

"No, actually Tom Cochrane."

"Charlie, I didn't know you listened to anything besides Roy Orbison."

"Hey even Roy joined a band and got on with his life after his son died. Thought I'd like something a little more modern and Tom, well, he is

Canadian, eh." He smiled with his impish grin. "After all I did get a Blue Jays ball cap to wear on fancy occasions."

"Like when you have your annual bath. Ah crap, how can I ever get mad at you?"

"It's the twinkle in my eye, the heart in my soul and the craziness in my veins. I think Tom sang that in one of his songs. Keeps you guessing?"

"That it does, mad shaman. That it does."

"Ah thanks for the compliment. You know how to flatter an old man."

"No funny ideas, I'm beginning to like hanging out with you and a pen full of murderers."

"Funny, like if you were to mix three badgers into a wrestling match with a wolverine and two amorous weasels, who'd end up on top? I think about that a lot."

"Yeah, exactly like that. Charlie it's a good thing I didn't meet you thirty years ago."

"Because you'd be six and I'd get charged for child molestation."

"NO, nut job, because I'd arrest you for lunacy and have you locked up tight in the loony bin."

"Well thank you. I'm truly honoured."

"Grrr, no more wise cracks. I've had enough." Carol strode off toward the prison. "Let's go to your office and see if I can get into Ken's computer. I'm still surprised that you even managed to turn it on."

"Me too!"

* * *

I'm not alone. There are others alive. Others I can talk to. Talk, I haven't talked in a long time.

He let out a shrill burst of sound, the ground trembled and the air sizzled.

No I can't talk here. I am trapped to think in my head only. I must reach again.

* * *

"Okay," Carol turned on the computer. "Now, pass me your mouse."

"My ferret."

"Pardon me?"

"Mouse wasn't right so I named him Ferret. He looks sleeker and he's way faster than a mouse."

"Because they're always ferreting around looking for things. Got it."

"And as you can see, ex mousy here doesn't like cheese."

Carol stared at the crumbs of dried cheese bits beside the mouse. "You drive me nuts."

"That would be squirrels."

"It's only called a mouse."

"Well my tested theory just proved that."

Carol shook her head. "They were originally wired to computers and someone thought they looked like a mouse with a long tail, hence the term. Now, his computer is password protected. So trusting what most people use and accepted government protocol." She typed in his last name. "Bingo."

"Genius. I knew I brought you here for a reason."

Carol opened up the section with his folders. "He kept folders of…"

She opened one titled Sweats. "Each sweat." She opened one up and then another. "Apparently keeping detailed notes on each participant and what he discovered during the sweat." Carol opened the last entry up. "This is the sweat before the last one. Interesting the same participants and…" She read quietly for a moment.

"Hey there's two of us here."

"Sorry, I'll read it out. 'It had been a full moon, cloudless night when we entered the sweat. I decided to do something different and perform a group hypnosis as most participants have issues with their past childhoods. Thinking I could regress everyone back to release the horrors they went through or at least find a place where they can come to grips with what happened. Only at one point when thunder and lightning shook the grounds, I stopped."

"He stopped because a storm was brewing," Charlie interjected.

"What you've missed is the beginning, which didn't start with Snoopy sitting on his doghouse typing, 'It was a dark and stormy night."

"Oh yeah." He scratched under his ball cap. "You're pretty clever at deducing. Ever think of being a cop?"

"I am one. Now let me read on, or I will take my truncheon to you. 'I managed to bring everyone out of it quickly. But I've stirred something that was deeply hidden in the subconscious of one of them. What and who is a deeper mystery. Will reform the group in two weeks and try again, this time I'll be better prepared. Need to study some material in order to deal with this bizarre turn of events.'" She paused.

"And?"

"That's it except for the fact he mentions that when they exited the tent he could see all the stars in the night sky." Carol sat quietly waiting for the normally chatty shaman to say something glib. Only he didn't. "So, no thoughts, oh mystical one?"

"Might explain the ancient writing on the walls and the fact that a couple of them have gone a little more wacko since then. But I'm not liking the thunder and lightning thing. This doesn't bode well."

"Especially since he got killed for exposing something he wasn't meant to find."

"I think no one was ever meant to find what he uncovered and whatever that was, he paid a heavy price. So whatever this is, it wants to be kept very hidden." The usually chipper shaman frowned.

"I would agree. I think we need to sit down and question everyone separately and then we'll cross examine what each has said." Carol added.

"I think I need to go to the washroom, but agreed. This is like a real Agatha Christie mystery." He shuffled towards the door. "Should be right up your alley."

"What would be up my alley is a smoke and lying on a nice hot beach with some hunky fireman. Okay let's get together after I talk to the warden and get the inmates rounded up."

* * *

The shaman was here. The other was here. There must be a way out?

Chapter Eight

She stood in the clearing and lit another cigarette. *That native drives me crazy. So why do I put up with him?*

From the corner of her eye she caught the slight sway in a dark bunch of bushes. *Is it?*

An eye blinked and some ferns waved slightly.

Yeah, I am being watched again.

Why is it that I can see whatever that is? Or does it want me to? Hm. Let's try this. Two can play this game. She grabbed a few twigs from the grass around her and bent them into the shape of a person. Carol put it on the ground and scratched a happy face symbol on the ground beside it. *Now let's see if you want to communicate.*

With that she butted out her smoke and walked slowly away without so much as glancing back.

* * *

Charlie entered Bryan's cell the next day. "I just wanted to see if the potion I brewed up is working, not sure how long it will take." Bryan stared at him. He wasn't muttering and able to focus somewhat on his visitor. "Well at least it seems to have settled you. Now I'm going to try and put you into a trance or at least quieten you some more so that we can see what's going on inside."

Charlie sat cross-legged before Bryan and made him do the same. He held his hands in his own and the two began to breathe deeply and slowly.

Once he knew Bryan had reached a meditative state, Charlie opened his eyes.

"So Mr. Fog Eight, better known as Mumbles, you knew the plane went down and, more impressive, you knew I'd see the paper that published that article for me to read. So how are you doing this and what do you see today?"

Bryan stared blankly at Charlie. "Fish, big fish swimming by." He blinked. "Ocean shore." He blinked several times. "Now green forest, carpet under my feet. I stalk quietly, my prey waits. . ." Bryan turned his head. "I'm seen."

He hesitated and shook his head staring blankly, "Gone. It's gone." He began to rock back and forth. Charlie knew he'd gone somewhere else in his head. Whatever that vision was, didn't want to be seen. "Okay, let's calm down again and…"

Bryan began to whisper what sounded like words. Songlike.

Charlie leaned in, the words familiar. "I was all right for a while. I could smile for a while. But I saw you last night, you held my hand so tight." Bryan looked up at him and smiling added, "As you stopped to say 'hello'."

"How do you know those words?" It was from Crying, One of Charlie's favourites by his favourite singer, Roy Orbison.

"Woman dying, in my arms."

Charlie's eyes widened before he closed them. He got it. His deepest memory, the song he sang when he held her as she died. "That's the song I sang as I held her, held ..."

"Lucy," they both whispered together.

"How do you know?"

Bryan didn't respond, instead he muttered, "Charlie, my love, I shall wait for you on the shore."

Her words, the last she spoke as she died. Words he'd never forget. He snapped his fingers bringing Bryan out of hypnosis. "You, my friend, are not crazy."

Bryan glared at him. "I see things, all the time. In my head. I get these, here." He pounded his head.

"I know you do. Doesn't make you schizo. You have the rare gift, one that the whites don't understand. I can see why you were diagnosed the way you were." He leaned forward on his cane and stared deep into the troubled man's eyes. They flitted back and forth.

"Help me. Others have called me crazy my whole life. I thought they were right. I thought myself crazy. So much goes on inside, can't stop it." He said, his eyes clearing again.

"Oh no, you're saner than me and that is saying a lot. You, my good man are what the Haida call a Skaga, one that performs as a shaman, or in this case one that beholds. In the old days you'd have become like me, most probably, a shaman. You've a rare gift. The seeing through other's eyes and sometimes other's intimate objects."

"The what?" He rose agitated.

"You saw through my eyes. Saw my Lucy's death. You've seen through others as well, I'm sure."

"But I don't want to. It makes me crazy inside. So much." He stopped and pounded his fist on the wall. The guard outside reached for his keys. Charlie waved him off. "I've seen things, horrible things."

"I believe you have." He watched the man sob. "I reckon that spirits, whether you want them to or not, get inside your thick head." Charlie rose and bravely tapped the man on the side of the head with his finger.

"Not thick enough. They'd call me that in school. Thickhead." Tears ran down his face. “Please, can you help me?” He begged. “Don’t want the voices, the visions.”

“Ah, true gift is not appreciated if it is misunderstood, an old teacher once said. I think he was in the second Star Wars movie and I think his ears were bigger than yours.” Bryan smirked at him.

“I think I can help, but you must let me do whatever it takes. No matter how weird or bizarre it looks. And occasionally I’ll be asking for your help. We need to get you to control and understand this power.”

“My help Doc? I can’t help anyone.” He paused for a moment as one of the guards walked by. “Lightning dancing. Dancing away. Just dancing.” Charlie didn’t get a chance to see which guard walked by.

Lightning? Could it be he was the one that caused all the upheaval in the sweats?

“More odd things bouncing around in your head. Where did that come from?”

“Here, it all comes from here.” He slapped at his head. His scratches still scabbed over on his arms and the side of his face.

Charlie pulled his hands down. “Don’t! You don’t deserve it, don’t abuse yourself.” He held them as the man simmered down. “First of all it’s Charlie, and yes, you have a great deal that you can help others with. You already did by saving those left alive in that airplane. You’ve just got to begin to trust. First me, then yourself. Now tomorrow we’ll sit down and do this again. I’m making a potion that clears the mind and allows you to see better inside, to focus and hopefully decipher which thoughts are yours and which are from outside.

* * *

Carol strode into the outdoor grounds. All the female inmates were gathered on their break, non-smokers on one side and smokers the other. A haze drifted over everything. The guards patrolled quietly, watching carefully bored but still prepared for anything. She spotted the group she was interested in, three of the four women that had all been in the sweat Charlie was investigating. *Most funny coincidence.* Although she knew Charlie would have something different to say about that. Karmic and some such thing. *The only good thing about karmic is that it's good mixed in chocolate bars, like a Mars. Well time to introduce myself to the rabble and be prepared for the worst.* She put on a brave smile and approached the four. "Hey, how's it going?"

"Eat me, bitch." The short haired, oldest one of the group growled, staring at her.

"Yeah, got a problem with that, hate the taste of fishy things." She quipped back.

One laughed, the other flung her cig on the ground. "Police pond scum. I'd knife ya, if I had one."

"Probably why you're in here then." The short-haired butch glared back, obviously not used to being talked back to.

"You frigging read my file or something before coming here and trying to make small talk?"

"It's the or something. I won't shit you, Janice."

"Get it right, it's Jan or Ms. to you, screw."

Carol turned away from her, obviously ignoring her. "You're Florence and you're Cindy, her cellmate-slash-lover I take it."

"Yes," the second one quietly responded, finally speaking. The other two merely watched what was unfolding.

"And it's Flo," the short one of the two said. Obviously the more dominant.

"What's it to you? Gets a mite lonely at night and some of us do develop a taste for seafood after a while. Try it, you might enjoy it." She smiled. "You'd look good on your knees, naked, tongue hanging out."

Carol laughed. "Doubt it, but could be a switch from the palm sisters. Fingers tend to get a bit sore after a while."

They chuckled, except for the short-haired dyke, Janice, who, upset she'd been shut out of the conversation, walked off.

"Not one for small talk," Cindy said.

"Yeah, she's top dog around here. Mean as one too." Flo replied.

The look Flo gave her indicated that they'd had a fight before and things weren't settled yet.

"Obviously some around here have an attitude problem." Carol said.

"No, she just has a thing about the law. I think a few of us are in that same boat."

"Yeah, you guys are just the ones that got caught. The real trouble makers are still out there with even sicker attitudes. But sooner or later their asses will be bust and they'll be in here warming the bunks beside you."

The two stared at her like her butt was on fire or she was a Martian. "I have a little attitude too, but that's my job and I get paid quite well for it. Now about you two. Flo Davis and Cindy Smith, both of you were in the sweat where Ken Benson was murdered. Am I correct?" She didn't want to say much more, not wanting to reveal any more without revealing clues.

"We don't have to stand here and answer any of your questions. Come on, Cindy lets go stand where the air is a bit less foul." Flo walked off, Cindy obediently following.

Carol frowned for a minute. "Okay I apologize. I'm not trying to get your backs up here, just trying to solve a possible murder."

"Murder? Thought it was classified as a …"

"Work related incident. Not in my books. I know homicide when I see it. Now did you notice anything odd during that ritual?"

Cindy spoke up finally. "No, but I remember Silv…"

"Silvia Chartrell?"

"Yeah. She, like, began to blubber some weird language crap. I thought she'd had a stroke or something. I couldn't make, like, a word of what she said and, like, since then she hasn't been let out of her cell much. Gone snaky and I, like, hear that she spends half the night writing crazy things on her walls since then. Not normal."

"You think they'd simply take the damn chalk away." Carol answered, trying to dig a little deeper without appearing to do so.

"You'd think. Except, like, I heard when they did she used her own excrement and blood and feces to write with. Gave the chalk back, less smelly and easier to, like, clean up." She said as Flo came walking back.

"Thanks Cindy, I'll be back later if there's more questions."

"We ain't going anywhere," Flo joked.

"Also let Janice know that I want to talk to her as well."

"Wouldn't waste your breath. You'll get nothing out of her. Oh and Officer Ainsworth. We ain't ladies."

"Oh sorry, didn't mean to demean you."

"It ain't mean, just insulting." The two laughed.

* * *

They sat down after Bryan had ingested the brew Charlie brought him. Charlie took Bryan into another trance, to settle him down before opening his eyes and talking. He stared into Bryan's eyes. The man stared back, very focused for the first time since they met. "Welcome back. Now, let's test your limits. Does your gift, the beholding, extend to objects? You ever try to vision anything off an object?"

"Don't know, never tried." He spoke calmly, almost at peace and surprisingly articulate.

"Take my cane. I've had it most of my life, gifted to me from another older shaman when he died. He knew I was born to be a shaman and knew I'd need it. He was similar to yourself, a type of beholder, only all he could was see future events. I believe you can see much more."

Bryan picked it up and ran his hands along the knurled bark. He touched the Orca mounted at the top. "Nope, nothing." He stopped. "A crystal, placed inside the orca by a man about to die. But not from around here. European, he's from Europe. Oh god!" He dropped the walking stick. "Murdered! He was murdered."

"Impressive. I've done some research, it resided in a museum after being taken from a Haida town after it was wiped out by smallpox, before being repatriated. To the best of my knowledge, over in England someplace. Did know about the crystal, it is very powerful. Didn't know about the man. You have indeed some powerful ability there, my friend."

He smiled. "The crystal aids you sometimes." He paused. "Egyptian. Out of place, out of time. A man involved in the murder." He paused a moment. "Ice. Ice causes the death of many. He knows."

"Well, safe to say, this is new knowledge. I will have to investigate that at a later date."

"That's one of my gifts as you call it. It is supposed to aid me. It helps me to see things, which you see naturally through either your eyes, or your mind. I wonder which."

Charlie reached for the cane and swiftly tapped the man on the head with it.

"Oww, what the hell was that for." He rubbed his scalp.

"Safe to say it's your eyes through your mind. And it doesn't make you any smarter or more intuitive. Otherwise you'd have sensed that coming."

He rubbed his head. "Okay." Bryan shot two fingers in Charlie's direction and poked him in both eyes.

Charlie stumbled backwards, his eyes watering and he squinted several times, trying to focus. "Ow, what the heck was that for?"

"Funny, your gift doesn't make you any more intuitive either." They both began to laugh as Charlie rubbed back the tears in his eyes. Bryan rubbed the small lump forming on his head.

"Point, well made." The Shaman laughed.

"Thanks," he replied.

"For what, making me need glasses two years earlier? Didn't think this job came with danger pay along with medical." He rubbed at his eyes.

"No, for making me laugh. I haven't done that in years."

Charlie smirked back through his watery eyes. "Thanks. I think."

Bryan groaned and put his hands to his head. "Fish, big fish. Oh."

Charlie watched the fogginess begin to return. Whatever was in there was returning or whatever he'd been seeing was returning. He'd done enough for today. At least he knew the potion worked, even if just for a little while.

Bryan began to rock. "The lightning strikes." He whispered. "It strikes again and again."

He muttered as Charlie got up to leave. "If there's some way I can help you I will." He hadn't heard back anything regarding the man's parents yet. It was possible they'd already passed away.

* * *

Charlie sat down on the grass by the sweat lodge surrounded by several bundles of smudge. His medicine pouch lay open, several talismans lay in front of the shaman, his guardians, who stood on watchful duty as he fell into a deep meditative state. He knew when he was in a deep meditative state his body was helpless.

From outside looking in one could only see the native man cross-legged on the grass. Placing the cane across his knees he closed his eyes and allowed himself to pull away from his body, slipping down into the ocean's depths.

* * *

One guard left the grounds of the prison after he watched Charlie sitting in front of the sweat lodge. He got in his car and drove to the edge of the ocean. Making sure no one was around he stripped down until he was naked, left his clothes neatly folded under some rocks and dove headlong into the dark ocean waters of Hecate Strait. Before he hit the water his body shimmered and a brief flash lit the area. A long dorsal fin and flippers cut the water as he dove straight down into the ocean's depths, not once coming up for air.

* * *

Slipping from the bonds of this realm Charlie fell away from his body. Water, blue, surreal, swam by him as he sank into the ocean's depths until he stood on the still floor of what should be his Kushtaka's Village. Only as Charlie sand settled around him, he knew he'd be getting more questions than answers as a mangled bit of flesh, he took to be possibly a torso, floated by with little fish nibbling at the remains.

Nothing moved and destruction lay all around. Huts crumpled and destroyed, bodies partly decaying, fish nibbling at bits of flesh littering the sandy floor. Every hut destroyed into seagrass shreds. Bodies lay where they had been dismembered. Various entrails and blood fouled the waters. Utter devastation. Who did this?

Many heads torn from bodies off as if some kind of zombie-like terror, or a feeding frenzy, had ravaged everyone. He'd come to question his ex-power creature, the Kushtaka. Funny he never gave it a name.

Charlie moved slowly around, in this ethereal state nothing that had attacked this place could harm him. A flipper floated serenely by. *Who had done this and, the bigger question, why?* The Kushtakas, while basically peaceful, were feared by many around. They would take human prisoners and hold them hostage, slowly transforming their captives into versions of themselves, as the legends went. He couldn't smell anything in this state, which right about now might be a good thing, because in the open air above the stench of decay would be unbelievable. A part of a flipper floated by, bits of flesh torn away hung in the currents. Whatever had done this made sure that nothing remained intact. Even the young lay torn apart. If he had teeth, Charlie would have gritted them and, as if answering his thoughts

Help, rang out in his head. Charlie spun around in the water. Someone, his power animal, was alive. *Where?*

Large shell to west of village.

Charlie swam over and slowly willed himself to lift the clamshell. Under it, skin shredded as if by long jagged claws, head hanging limply, one eye torn out, his former helper. It was a wonder he'd lived this long.

What happened?

Attacked from nowhere, by…, he coughed blood. He wouldn't live long and had probably used nearly all of the strength it had left just to signal Charlie.

Blood flowed from most of his body, coating the sand. "I…"

Charlie interrupted. *No, think of an image, easier.*

The image of a fierce sea creature the world hadn't seen in many thousands of years filled his head. A creature that had vanished long ago. The sea wolf being, Wasgo.

The Kushtaka opened its eyes wide as its head fell backwards and his spirit slipped away in a wavy blur as it died. The shaman began to dig away a small grave and he deposited the body into it. He placed the shell above it and began to swim back to his body. *This was not good.*

I was afraid of this. Only why are they back? If it is why I think it might be then, there is one I need to find before it is too late. It was too late for the Kushtakas; as Charlie searched the other three villages that he knew of, he found much the same devastation. He rose back up through the dark waters flowing with the blood of these people. The Kushtakas didn't have many enemies and they usually kept to themselves. But he knew they never did get along with the Wasgo and were one of the few races that had any knowledge of these creatures. If they already knew about their return then the vile creatures were covering their tracks. *My friend, I will make sure your death is avenged.*

* * *

From between the tall seaweed two menacing eyes watched the shaman leave. His leader would need to know this and he'd have to be dealt with. None were supposed to know the Wasgo were back.

A low growl sank in its throat. The creature swam quickly to its master.

* * *

Carol watched the brush-cut Janice Jones walk towards her. Her nose had been mangled in the past, probably in one too many fights. A scar, probably from a knifing, trailed down the left side of her face.

"Okay, new screw. I hear you're looking for me. What's your problem, bitch?" She folded her arms in an obvious act of defiance with attitude.

Carol knew Janice, or Jan as she preferred to be called, was one of the tough ones who didn't take shit from anyone, even a guard. A tough nut to crack, if she even wanted to. "Well, it ain't because you're cute, but I do like the tattoo." She spotted the killer whale just below her left ear disappearing under her prison garb.

"I make my bottoms lick it at night when I'm doing them. Gives me strength. Want to lick it yourself?" she smiled and parted her lips. Carol figured her smiling was pretty rare and the parting of the lips was a sign of sexual arousal.

Yeah, a crazy one here. Six feathers short of a headdress, as Charlie would say. "Good thing I like it on top then but I don't think you got the right equipment for the job to satisfy me."

"What's your problem, bitch?" she snapped.

Obviously more the need-to–be-in-control type, than the conversational type. "You were in the sweat lodge when Ken was killed. I've a few questions."

"And I got nothing." She turned and walked away. "Except this." She gave Carol the finger behind her back.

"Yeah, love you too." *No, wouldn't get much out of that one without a lot of blood loss.*

Chapter Nine

Charlie signaled for the guard to unlock the cell. Bryan sat with his face in his hands, moaning again. "Too bad he doesn't ever get visions of numbers. We could have struck it rich on the next lottery draw." He smiled to the guard who took this as a sign to leave and strode down the hall but never out of earshot. Bryan grabbed the chalk and returned to scribbling over the walls. The potion hadn't cleared his mind today, which meant either he was becoming immune to it or something was trying to block him out. *I'll brew a stronger dose tomorrow.* "Don't know how yet, but we'll get you cured, or at least help control those visions, or I turn in my Shaman's union card."

* * *

The Wasgo carefully entered his leader's cave. "How dare you!"

"My leader, someone else knows of us," The normally hostile beast trembled; it knew the wrath of its master was great. It shared its thoughts.

"Well then, a shaman. The answer is simple. Track him down, and when he is alone, kill him. Or else." The Wasgo trotted out quickly. It didn't need to ask what the 'or else' meant.

I think it's time I joined the humans at the prison. Need to keep a closer eye on our amnesic friend.

* * *

Carol walked into Silvia's cell trying to read the remaining writing on the wall as one of the janitors washed it away. "Stop, please. I just need to document this." Carol readied the camera on her cell phone.

"Lady, I'm supposed to erase these before breakfast is over."

"Just give me a minute; I think Charlie would want to see these."

"But..."

"No buts or you'll be finding out how well soapy water and chalk suffice as an enema. I hear she used to use her own body fluids before they broke down and gave her chalk."

"She'd use her own feces and when that ran out, she'd claw herself and write in blood. It was horribly gross. We couldn't stop her so chalk seemed the better option," the janitor replied.

"I'll bet. It's as if she's being compelled from something inside her mind, seems to have no choice in the matter."

"No, just nuts. I've seen it before. We tried leaving it on the walls and she'd sit there jabbering away. Reading it over and over, out loud. Drove the others crazy." She glanced at her watch and, once Carol had finished, returned to the scrubbing with renewed effort.

"I ain't an English whiz kid. But I'd swear these look more like some kind of old language you'd see on the pyramids or on those rice paper or clay tablets," Carol said.

"Look I can't talk, gotta get this cleaned up quickly. I heard the warden and some fancy-pants professor dude talking one morning. He figured cuneiform or Easter Island language. Whatever that is. Now I gotta hurry." She sloshed a bucket of water over the walls, allowing the letters to melt away into the wet mess and grabbed her mop.

"Thanks, you've been most helpful." Carol shut off her phone's camera and left. She needed to show this to Charlie.

* * *

Charlie stared at the pictures as they stood at the back of the grounds. "Wow, your phone takes pictures like this? My old Polaroid didn't take pictures this good."

"Polaroid? I think they went bankrupt twenty years ago. Charlie, all smartphones have built in cameras these days, along with GPS and Wi-Fi."

"Mine doesn't. What the hell is Wi-Fi and GPS?"

"Charlie your land line phone is an old rotary dial up. I think there's more in museums than there are in use these days." She explained what the two terms were.

"Hmm, you think I should, like, try and update myself? Although I don't need locating technology, I usually know where I am and the spirits keep me in contact with what I need to know."

"No, it wouldn't be you. And another 'like', and I will brain you with my truncheon. One of the women in the pen speaks like that and it drives me mad. What got you started?"

"I'm trying to be hip and trendy, what with my new 'puter skills and all."

"Well, stop. It's not hip and trendy just shows you don't really know what to say next. What do you make of these?" Carol returned Charlie's attention to the pictures.

"Well I recognize some of these symbols. So whatever is affecting the Beholder, is also doing it to Silvia." He quickly explained to Carol all he'd learned from Bryan.

"So I'm to assume that something is blocking or addling their minds on purpose?"

"Yes, and I'm going to say it has to do with Ken's death. I think he got too close to something he shouldn't have. That's why I'm going to convince the warden to do another sweat with everyone from the last one, with me in charge."

"What? Are you crazy? What if you get killed too?"

"I think the warden would be a mite happy about that. Could get you in there as well, helps purify the spirit?"

Carol shivered. "I usually use whiskey for that."

"Yes, that is exactly why you need to do a sweat. If you want to know better who did this, you need to get into their head."

"Get into a very hot sweaty tent, surrounded by people who are perspiring some, present company not excepted, maybe have only used bark leaves in the last few years to wash with and no weapons? There's a few in that crowd that would either like to get me in the dark and feel me up or throttle me. It ain't gonna happen."

"Let's see. What did I learn the other day about police procedure? Re-enact the crime as accurately as possible and something is bound to turn up."

"I gotta get you away from those damn computers, you're getting too darn smart for that already swollen head." Carol snickered.

"I'm telling ya, Google doesn't lie."

Carol moaned, "I've created a computer shaman geek. Okay if you can convince the warden, I'm in. But I think you wanting to re-enact the sweat would be like The Seventh Calvary wanting to redo the Little Big Horn except only the natives are allowed to have live ammo."

* * *

"So I've checked out your file. I'm sorry neither of your parents are still alive. You stayed with your uncle, Jimmy Wilson, for the last two years before you were put into residential school." Charlie spoke.

Bryan's face went cold. "That bastard, very cruel. He beat me silly."

"You don't want to meet up with him then? Stand up to him? I'll be there with you." Charlie had read Ken's notes on the things Bryan had shared with him. The man had tortured and molested him.

Bryan looked up at him with a youngster's hurt eyes, brimming with tears. "I can't."

"You must. If we are to get you to heal and get on with your life, you must. Do you want the memory of what he did to you forever inside?"

Bryan rocked back and forth, mumbling to himself. Charlie was afraid he'd lose him again. "Bring the Big Mountain along and I will."

He began to sob and mutter incoherently. Obviously going to some dark place inside. Charlie got up to leave, there wasn't any more he could say or do today.

* * *

"Now, ever interrogated anyone?" Carol asked. Carol had decided to interview all of the sweat participants before they scheduled the next, hoping to get more information out of them. Especially as to why they had two writing weird ancient languages on their cell walls.

"Can't really say I have. Although the librarian at my local library asked me what I thought of the recent changes in the library. Does that count?"

"Grrr, no. I'm talking about trying to get information or the truth out of someone. A police interview."

"Nope, that's why you've got the badge and I've got the walking stick, which I'd just use to whack them upside the head and yell 'talk, before I shove this somewhere you're not going to like'."

"No, that's the old days of interview methods. Today, you try to befriend them and get them to trust you."

"Oh, I like the whacking idea. Worked in my backyard when I cornered a bunch of squirrels. But befriend them, don't think that works with squirrels, other than the topic of nuts they aren't much in the way of conversationalists. Mind you they've got every angle of that subject covered."

"Charlie!" She could visualize him with half a dozen squirrels all tied up, alternating questions with taps on the head. "Now remember, befriend him. Get him on our side."

"Okay." They walked into the interview room. Charlie smiled ear to ear as he walked in and sat opposite Eddie Stone. Carol shook her head, noting she shouldn't let him smile ever again. Made him look rather possessed, but then, he was. "So, Eddie, how's the wife and kids?"

"Ain't got any." He sat with his arms crossed in a defensive posture.

"Oh sorry about that. How's work? What was it you did for a living before you ended up in here?"

"Rob banks."

Charlie frowned. "Okay, how about those Canucks?"

"Don't watch TV. I'm in jail and I hate hockey."

"Blue Jays?"

"Hate baseball." He crossed his arms tighter.

"Okay now that we're on a best bud level, where were you on the night of the eighteenth of last month between the hours of ten and midnight."

"Well in the sweat obviously."

Carol interrupted. "Charlie; outside."

Carol scolded Charlie as they stood outside the interview room. "They were all in the sweat. Don't even think of asking that again."

"Well, a good officer I happen to know said never to assume. I thought that's what you told me?" He looked at her puzzled.

"Yeah, but that's bleeding obvious."

"Yes, but as you said I want to see the response in their eyes."

"You are such a whack job."

"Sto:lo."

"What?"

"My Sto:lo native cousins live in the whack, Chilliwack. It's in the Fraser Valley, near…"

"I know where bloody Chilliwack is. I should give you a true whack upside the head. And yes, as infuriating as you are, the rules of investigation are 'never assume'. Where did you learn that from?"

"Watch a lot of CSI: Haida Gwaii."

"What? You're kidding me."

"The Canadian version of the show obviously. Great theme music. Instead of those British blokes…"

"The Who?"

"Yeah, I don't know who either. Still 'Won't Get Fooled Again' but done in smoke signals."

Carol giggled, "Let me guess; the acoustic version, native style."

"Oh, you're starting to get all of my jokes."

"Hanging out with you far too long. I gotta get me a fireman and…"

"Blah, blah, blah." He covered his ears. "Don't want to know anything about firemen and their hoses thank you very much."

"How about we stick to the questioning? Now back inside."

After a few minutes Carol tapped Charlie on the shoulder again. "Eddie, give us a minute. Charlie come with me please."

"Give me a mo', bro, the ball and chain calls."

She dragged him outside by the collar. "Charlie, I said befriend him."

"I think I'm softening him up. He's ready to spill his guts."

"The only thing he's going to spill is his dinner if he got food poisoning and his social insurance number, and we already know that." Carol shook her head. "Why couldn't I just say no and just be relaxing on the beach right now. Okay we go back in together and not a word out of you. I'll lead, you listen and learn."

"Listen and learn, check, got it, memory forever, message received and zero distortion."

"One hundred percent distortion." Carol moaned, how many times had he said that line before all hell broke loose and went sideways.

"I'll be honest. His body language indicates that he's closing up. You're not helping, but hindering this investigation, Charlie. Now when we go back inside, I want you to sit quietly and observe. Not a bloody peep out of you, or any smartass comments."

"But…"

"Not even a frigging 'but'. If you can't agree, I'll do this on my own. Got it?"

"Yes sir, Aye, aye sir. Message received, zero ..."

"Don't even think of going there again. I'm very serious here. We've a killer on the loose and little over a week to get him." She glared harshly at him.

"Did I ever say you're cute when those cheeks go all red like that?"

"Not one comment like that. Now watch a pro in action and learn something. The art of the interview is part of my training and I'm very good at it."

She opened the door quietly and put her notepad in front of her as she sat down opposite Eddie. "If it's okay, I'll be taking some notes while we talk."

"Do what the hell you want." Carol noted his posture, which was sitting with his legs crossed, closed up, and as he saw Charlie, he folded his arms in front of himself. Charlie sat two chairs over from Carol.

"Okay, sorry about that Eddie. Charlie here is having a bad day, someone substituted his Wheaties for Corn Flakes and he just found out his entire life savings, all forty bucks that he invested in Smudge Grass bonds, has just tanked."

He smiled. "I'm surprised the bastard has that kind of money to invest," he growled with a sardonic sneer on his face. But Carol caught his arms beginning to relax.

"So tell me about yourself. Judging by the calluses on your hands, you look like a hard-working man."

He unfolded his arms and looked at his palms before putting them on the table. "Not much to tell you. I worked in the Alberta oilfields for a while. Came back here with a load of cash and blew it all on booze and women. Decided to become a logger instead."

"You like that more?"

"Yes. Being alone in the forest surrounded by vegetation that doesn't talk back is a lot better than being coated in crude."

Carol caught the reference to not talking back and jotted it in her notes. She was quite surprised by Charlie who was indeed just sitting back and observing. He didn't look like he was angry with her upfront comments, but more open to watching and learning. *As much as he drives me crazy, I gotta admire the guy for taking his lumps and sticking with it.* "I guess I'd rather be covered in bark and tree sap than gooey oil."

"Easier to wash off." He leaned forward, she'd caught his interest. He was now open to questions.

"Now if you don't mind me asking, what got you here? I haven't seen your file and don't know anything about you."

Eddie looked hard at Carol. "A woman and the booze. I got good and drunk one night. Too drunk. My girlfriend started some silly argument and back chatted me."

"You don't like someone back talking to you." Charlie gave a slight cough. The look on his face told her that he'd just caught his main mistake with his methods earlier.

"No, my dad would back hand us kids if we ever talked back to him. He was the boss. What he said goes." Eddie eyes began to mist. "I hit her too hard, she called the RCMP and I lost it when she started chucking stuff at me. I began smacking her around as the cops came in."

He grew quiet. Carol gave him a moment as he struggled to find the words. For all she knew this could have been the first time he ever admitted his guilt. "Sad part was, I didn't even remember hitting her the last time. When the cops got there she was laying in the corner bleeding and barely conscious. They tackled me and I went nuts, beat the crap out of a couple before they handcuffed me and took me down. She died before the ambulance got there." He hung his head down.

"They gave you ten years for battery and assault."

"Yeah, deserved it. The only good thing is that I haven't touched the bottle since and won't when I get out of this shit shack."

"You miss her then?" She decided to probe his emotions.

"Yeah, the only good thing in my world and I wrecked it." He looked straight at her. "I can tell you I ain't touching another bottle ever again." Carol could tell by the look in his eyes that he was telling the truth.

"I know how you feel. When I was in my early twenties, my woman died in my arms. I loved her more than anything." They both looked at Charlie, virtually forgetting he was still in the room. Carol caught a tear tremble down his face. It was the first time she seen him emotional, never realizing he had a tender side.

Shockingly Eddie replied, "Sorry to hear that man."

"Yeah, same with you." Carol was prepared to cut Charlie off if he went into some of his personal stuff, but didn't need to. He just sat there.

While he was vulnerable Carol decide to wade in. "Now, what do you remember about the night Ken Benson died in the sweat?"

Eddie looked up and to the right. She knew he was searching his memories and it was coming from truth. "Oddly not much. It ended much like the first one. Ken was beginning to put some of us into a relaxed state when the ground began to shake. I thought I heard something whizz by me as thunder and lightning broke across the sky. A storm, a real one was brewing."

"Real one?"

"Yeah, the first time I thought it odd that when we got out the sky was clear. Thought maybe a storm coming."

"Then what?" Charlie asked. She had him back from his memories.

"I vaguely remember him yelling 'everyone out'. Not that we took much telling, none of us wanted to stay inside anyways. It felt like electric snakes were crawling all over us. Was real panic and confusion, all of us trying to get out the small opening of the lodge at the same time, everyone scratching and swiping at themselves like they were covered in ants or something. One of the guards ran off."

"Do you know which one?"

"Adam, I think. Although maybe not because he took us back to the prison. Dunno really. With all the hoo-ha I may have imagined it."

Carol kept scribbling in her notebook as he talked, Charlie listening intently.

Charlie asked, "Anything else?"

"Yeah. I remember one of the women whispering into a guard's ear. I vaguely thought that odd."

"Was that Adam or the other one that you thought ran off?"

"Not sure. Not sure there even was another one now. Like I say, total confusion with the thunder and lightning, pissing rain and everyone panicking about being covered in ants or something."

"Which woman and why odd?" Carol backtracked.

"Don't know her name. The dyke with the short hair, busted nose. Jan, I think." He said rudely. "Odd in the sense that she was the one squawking the loudest about being stung by lightning."

"That is odd. Then what happened?"

"All I remember is us running across the grounds. Pissing down, thunder and lightning slamming around us, like I said. Guards came out the prison to guide us in, make sure we were all there like, and as I entered the building I saw one go into the sweat lodge."

"Did you catch who?"

"No, just saw the back of him. I guessed at the time that he was just securing the tent flaps, which were being chucked around."

Carol tapped her pen on her pad. "Remember anything else?"

Eddie thought a moment. "Only that I thought it funny that shortly after we entered the jail cells, the storm seemed to settle down and before I knew it the rest of the night was quiet."

"Okay thanks. You can go and we'll call the next one in, in a minute."

"Crap lady, you're good, you even had a tear out of me." Charlie said quietly to Carol as Eddie walked out.

"Thanks, but I'm beginning to see something developing here. We need to see if anyone else noticed what he did or if their stories back him up. I get the sense that he was talking the truth. Although odd about a second guard, I thought only Adam was posted on that duty."

"Guards can come and go without an escort you know. Oh and the truth is it was smudging bowls that I lost my forty dollars in. Thought I'd make a small fortune."

Carol shook her head. He'd never change and as much as he drove her mad, she really didn't want him to. Not that she'd ever admit that to Charlie. She nodded to the guard to let the next one in.

* * *

Why am I here? Alone? I have been here a long time. So long I don't remember. What I did before or if there was a before? But there must have been. I wasn't born here, did I have parents? Or brothers? Or friends? Friends...

Something twigged inside.

I... remember...I had friends that is why I am here?

* * *

Charlie and Carol sat in the room after the last interview was done. She looked at the blank pad before the shaman. "Okay let's talk and compare about what we learned while I go back through my notes." She flipped through the pages.

"I didn't need notes. It's all here." He tapped the cane to his forehead.

"I'm afraid to see what's in there."

"Now no one else but Eddie mentioned the whistling noise and he sat next to Ken."

"So it's possible the target may have been Eddie and not Ken? Unless Eddie killed him, but I doubt that since only he mentioned the noise and why would he do that if he whacked Ken in the head? Which in the mass confusion as everyone scrambled to exit the sweat lodge wouldn't be too hard to do." Carol thought out loud.

"Agreed," Charlie replied. "It is possible that they wanted to stop Eddie because of whatever was inside him, except he's probably one of the more normal ones in this group. Bryan, Thomas, even Griz, I could agree with."

"Agreed, along with Jan and Silvia. So it could have been Eddie that was the target instead of Ken, unless they wanted to get him anyway, since whatever he was doing was treading on something not meant to be discovered."

"Then you'd think maybe they'd also want to kill off the one Ken was upsetting, for lack of a better term."

"If he or she can be killed."

"WHAT?" Carol retorted, completely thrown off her line of thought.

"I don't have answers yet, but if I'm right I think I know why they'd not want this being trapped inside someone waking up."

"Are you crazy? Ah, let me rephrase that, because I know you are." Carol stared at her notes a minute. "Okay, the woo-woo crazy stuff is way out of my league, that is your field. I can and will only stick to the facts in front of me. So don't tell me anymore. At this point I think we have enough proof to go to the warden. And we need to have Adam the guard stationed brought in for questioning."

Charlie stared blankly for a moment. "Agreed." He finally blurted. *Although I get that there is much more here than meets the eye.*

* * *

Charlie opened the flap to the elaborate duck blind that was set up half a kilometer from the prison and walked in on two young white males who were busy beginning to load plastic wrapped cylinders of white substance into what looked like an army ordinance mortar. It had a clear line of fire downhill to the rear of the penitentiary. “Hello fellas. Nice duck blind you’ve got here.”

The two, dressed in ball caps, black hoodies and pants hanging down around their knees, stared blankly at him.

“Only I think we’ve a problem around here. First of all it’s the off season and by the looks of that bazooka thing, you’re hunting some damn big birds. Would that be an Ostrich or a Dodo gun?”

“Hey, old man. Don’t know how the fuck you got out here or found us, but piss off. The only dodo around here is going to be you joining the rest of those extinct motherfuckers if you don’t beat it.” He pulled out his pistol as a rank smell filled the air. The other man also reached for own his gun as he pinched his nostrils.

“Just off the bastard. We don’t have time for this kind of shit.” The other snarled, looking under the covers to make sure no one else was around.

From behind them two hairy arms reached out and wrenched their weapons away. “What the…”

“God, it stinks.”

A growl filled the air as Bigfoot stood up, his head swelling the canvas upwards. They stared at the bulk of the eight foot massive beast behind them as it pitched the pistols through the awning and let out a roar.

Charlie walked over and looked in the large box they were unloading. “Now, as far as I know this time of year ducks don’t normally fly in the direction of the jail. They are going more of a southern route. And these.” He sniffed. “Don’t look like any kind of buckshot I know of.”

“Now time for a little chat and don’t make a move to escape. I’ve a rather hungry black bear sitting by your truck.”

A loud growl pierced the air and the sound of metal being scraped stung their ears. He picked up the pouches of white and stared at the two stunned young men. “Quite the elaborate setup, this duck blind. But, no duck hunting licences then. Tsk, tsk. So I think I’ll have to decommission the evidence then won’t I before any innocent avian type creatures get injured, don’t you think?” The Sasquatch grabbed the mortar and with a loud grunt bent the muzzle into a severe angle.

The two boys’ eyes bulged and they began to shake in fear. “Now, those pants of yours are just a bit ridiculous. Did you know where the low slung pants thing began? In jail oddly enough. It was a way for the more, shall I say rainbow orientated guys to advertise to any prospective males, that they were open for business. Now, lucky for you cute looking boys I’m more into - how d’you call it? –hos myself. But Chewbacca’s uncle here, he’s not so picky on what he humps himself.”

The two went white as they spotted the enormous appendage beginning to swell up from the grunting Sasquatch. The sound of dribbling water broke the air. “Looks like you two could use some pampers. Oh, he is called Bigfoot, but no one’s seen him aroused or I think we could agree he’d be called big-something-else.”

Wetness spread across the front of both males as four eyes widened in imagined horror. “Now, I think he finds you two boys rather yummy and what you don’t know is the smell of urine lets him know you’re responsive to his advancements. Funny creatures, Sasquatches are, don't take no for an answer very well. So if you two aren't into some rumpy-pumpy I'd suggest you beat it before he takes a shining to you. NOW."

Charlie stepped aside and let the pair trip over themselves as they ran outside, clawing at their pants trying to keep them up.

They fell into each other as they stared at their jacked up Dodge four-by-four. Large claw marks and jagged deep scratches ran down the side. A black bear grunted as it lifted its leg and sprayed the truck and them. "Oh, in case you ever decide to return, my buddy Blackie here is merely marking his territory. Likes to know what his next meal is going to be."

They screamed in terror as they scrambled into their vehicle. The oversized tires tore at the ground as they spun off across the field.

"Man, not the first blind date that hasn't gone well."

Chapter Ten

James looked up from his desk as Charlie entered. "You want me to let you take him outside?"

"Yes sir. It's in order to heal him. I've dug into the records, both his parents have passed away and he needs to meet the man that abused him. He'll get the chance to finally speak up for himself. To heal. To right some of the wrongs. Isn't that what prison is about? Paying your debts and trying to make these inmates better and whole?"

James dropped his face into his hands. "I heard what you did with Thomas Johnson. I really can't authorize this." He stared long and hard at the shaman. "But I hear what you're saying and I know from what I've seen you do, Charlie Stillwaters, that you are a man of good intentions and have some kind of healing gift I've never seen before but, again, I can't authorize this." Charlie's face sagged. "Not unless another guard and I accompany you. That is the only legal way I can allow this."

Charlie's face lit up. "He wants the Griz along with us too. Don't know why, maybe protection or courage to do this."

"What? Thomas Johnson is one massive man."

"This man is absolutely terrified of confronting his tormentor and I've a hunch it would help Thomas as well to watch someone go through hell. Maybe we could cure two for the price of one."

James breathed deeply. "Charlie?"

"You know I'm right."

"That's the problem. Okay. Do it. I'll figure out what kind of legal paper work to file this under. But Thomas stays in cuffs and two guards will accompany us or no deal."

"Done." Charlie began to walk out.

"Oh and Charlie."

"Save your breath. It'll be shoot first and ask questions later. Man, do I know you or what?"

"Get the hell out."

"You won't regret this, sir boss man, sir."

"I already do." He reached into his desk to pop two Aspirins for the massive headache that was erupting.

* * *

Charlie sat meditating by the sweat lodge. He'd been sensing it all week. His wolf power animal growled as he stood guard. *Yes, I sense that too. Something out there is watching me and it ain't Ghyldeptis. Much darker than that. I think I need to weave a spell to protect myself and take a little walk through the woods tomorrow.*

The Bigfoot and the others grunted in response.

* * *

"I would like the same group as was in the sweat when Ken was murdered." Charlie said as he spoke to Carol at the back of the pen.

"Are you crazy?"

"Yup. It's the only way I can think of flushing out the killer, like a true Herry K Parrot."

"I think you mean Hercules Poirot." Carol laughed.

"Yeah, that's what I meant. My French is a little rusty, well except for poutine. I like Poutine. Made with French fries. Although oddly enough I do believe that they never invented them."

"Right, it was the Belgians. Poirot was Belgian too."

"Belgian. Really? Always thought he was French, same as the fries. What about the Belgian waffles then; were they French? Oh, you whites are a confusing lot."

"Charlie you are off the wall nuts. But I'm prepared to back you up."

"Hey have I ever been wrong?" he said, as they walked towards the warden's office.

Carol looked at him like his pants were on fire. "Okay, much. Have I ever been wrong much?"

They banged on the warden's door and entered. "I know you granted me a special day pass for Bryan and Griz, but I've decided I want to re-enact the sweat again. With the same group."

"Enough," the warden barked as he glared at Carol and Charlie. "Outrageous. I can't approve this. I have already bent my rules once Charlie Stillwaters." His voice raised about ten decibels. "And now you want me to break them again. What if something should happen? I've already got one man's death on my hands. I don't want the death of a second Elder on my hands."

"And I thought you didn't like me. That's sweet of you to worry. But I can look after myself and the killer would be only after me and no one else. Besides I've my trusty cane, wits and I boned up on a little Tai Chi the other day. I can defend myself." He moved his one hand like he was doing a karate move. Carol looked skyward.

The warden looked at Charlie with disdain as an evil smile broke his face. "You know what, thinking again, I agree. It could be a splendid way to flush out the killer. Only on one condition and that's you and you alone join the group. I think recreating the crime scene in exact detail except with Charlie replacing the victim. Are you up for it? Carol will have to be stationed outside to frisk everyone before going in. When do you want it arranged?"

Charlie only had to think a second. "Next Tuesday. Oh, wardy baby, and here I thought you truly had begun to care about me. I may have to lodge a complaint of harassment with the Union about this. I've been reading up on the Union rule book the other night as well. Rather stuffy reading but I didn't see any good thrilling Agatha Christie's, True Romance or Lone Ranger novels. Why is it that Tonto always had to do the dirty work and 'Ah Plenty Bad Kemosabe' which, by the way, sounds like a rather tasty Sushi dish, got all the glory. I reckon he had a really bad acting contract in the days when the cavalry was always the white guys. Thanks James. I won't let you regret it," Charlie said, as he reached for the doorknob to walk out with Carol.

"I'm beginning to say this a lot, but I already do. Only, you're not in the Union yet. Can't join until after I decide your probationary period is over."

"And when might that be?"

"Twenty-nineteen, at the earliest, if I can help it. Which would be the year after I put in for early retirement," the Warden replied in exasperation as Charlie and Carol left the room.

"Do you get that he really doesn't like me?"

"Hate, can't stand, detest are probably closer to the truth. You really shouldn't bait him so much. It would make your life and a possible pension entitlement here a little bit easier." Carol shook her head. She was always of the belief you never talk back to your boss, because even if he's wrong he's still the boss. "And you may need him for a reference in the future."

"Yeah, but he's such fun to bug, white collar stiffness and all. Takes himself too serious, needs to lighten up. I'll bet he doesn't get laid much at home." Charlie snickered.

"Oh, you're bad. So Tuesday we re-enact the sweat. Any idea who the killer is yet? If you live until Tuesday, and why Tuesday?"

"Wasn't it Jughead that said I'll pay you Tuesday for a hamburger today?"

"I think it was actually Wimpy from Popeye." She laughed. "You really do watch too much TV."

"Hey, no wife, only little animals to talk to out in my backyard and the odd spirit creature that stops by for coffee to gripe about the weather or the fact that his wife ran off with Casper the really friendly but well-endowed ghost. Yeah, a guy definitely gets bored."

Carol just shook her head laughing, wondering if he ever thought about taking stand-up comedy as a backup trade.

* * *

"Now, you're really going to go into a sweat lodge, with a suspected killer all by yourself? You are nuts."

"Well, only one killer."

"That we know of. And I won't be allowed in. I can only keep watch outside."

"I'll be careful, I have some friends of my own to protect me."

"Oh, those weird power animal things you've told me about. They are for real?"

"Carol, there's a few secrets I haven't told you about. Mainly because I know you wouldn't believe me or think I'm crazy."

"Oh, I knew you were crazy eighteen seconds after we first met."

"And you're still hanging out with me?"

"It's called 'due to circumstances beyond my control.' As soon as this is done I'm off to the nearest beach, get myself a few beers, a hot stud and go back to enjoying my holidays. But you will be careful?"

"Is that a smidge of concern, Mrs. I-don't-give-a-rats-ass-about-you?"

"Hey, I don't. Just, you know, a little concerned."

"Got it. I've been known to grow on a lot of people."

Carol shook her head. "So does old age and menopause and I don't like either of those."

Charlie smiled as he twirled his cane. *Whatever is out there is watching us and I'm not picking up good vibes.*

* * *

Charlie walked through the forest just behind the prison. He was missing a herb for Bryan's potion, Lemon Balm, which although prefers dry climates, and the West Coast of Canada is anything but, he'd seen some on one of his earlier walks through the forest. Something he often did, in search of plants to make some of his potions. He'd already had the prison order in Roseroot, which is very effective on brain clarity, grows only in Canada's coastal and alpine regions. This new batch of tea would make the effects stronger and hopefully keep Bryan better focused when they went to see his uncle Jimmy, which he knew was not going to be easy on the beholder and most likely put him into the deep end and out the other side.

He stopped suddenly. What he called his 'Spidey sense' was going crazy. Something was here and it wasn't good. He barely got the cover off the medicine pouch when this great wolf like creature burst from the woods. It leaped by him, claws raking the shaman down his side and disappeared again into the bushes. Charlie clutched at his side, blood streaming down. *Crap, my best shirt. Actually my only shirt.* "That my friend was a mistake, should have took me down then and there. But then you're a predator, a hunter that enjoys the stalking. Building the fear on my blood. I was counting on that." To any onlooker Charlie was babbling to himself but he knew he was heard.

Yes. Answered from the woods. *But, that blow was meant to kill you instantly not maim you. How did I miss?*

"Well, I think you picked the wrong fella. As you can see by my trusty cane I ain't a runner. Detest marathons and don't even own a pair of runners." As he talked Charlie called out to his animal spirits. "I wove my spell earlier when I began to detect your presence watching me out here. The spell is similar to what some natives call the bulletproof spell. Worked for Geronimo. This one displaces your perception of where I'm standing."

Then prepare to die. The wolfen-like beast burst from the woods. It had an orifice on its back just behind its head and small fins attached to the back of its legs.

Ah, as the ancient drawings of Bryan's foretold. The Wasgo have returned. Only why? Is the question.

Charlie neatly side stepped the creature's lunge, its claws raking only thin air, and with his cane tripped the large creature. It tumbled head-over-heels screaming its rage.

"My, testy are we? Or haven't you eaten in quite a while. "

I ate. I ate some of your guardians. Delicious. And you shall join them. Now prepare to surrender to my jaws and fill my belly. The creature lunged at Charlie only to get hammered to the ground. Charlie's Sasquatch growled loudly and, beside him, the Black bear. His wolf being joined the group, although, the shaman noticed, with less desire than the others. *Probably something to do with the canine-like bloodlines.* The Wasgo got up and swiped at the bear as the Sasquatch lunged at it and got it into a head lock. "I was thinking it was your kind that killed my Kushtaka, with no mercy in cold blood."

This is a trap. You set me up.

"Not all is sometimes as it seems. The best part of reality is illusion."

This can't be. I am supposed to be hunting you.

"Yeah, well tell that to my Kushtaka friends before you slaughtered them all."

It struggled to break free of Bigfoot's grip as both beasts screamed their rage but couldn't. The Sasquatch was enjoying the wrestling match. It had been getting quite bored lately as Charlie's power animal and unlike what most people thought of the mythical animal it wasn't very docile.

Mercy! screamed the creature. It couldn't break free from the incredible strength of the elusive Bigfoot. The black bear crushed one leg in its jaws. Blood spurted over all of them.

"Did you show Mercy to my Kushtaka or his family?"

I cannot I am a hunter.

"I can, but I swore I wouldn't."

Mercy.

"If I let you go you'll go back to your leader or turn on me and attack me. After all, you are a hunter and merciless at that." As much as Charlie wanted to save the vile creature, he knew letting it go would probably spell his demise, and, as of yet, he didn't want the leader knowing he was on to them. "Finish him off boys and don't leave any big pieces around for anyone to find."

Bigfoot twisted the Wasgo's neck hard and a loud crack resounded. All three of them tore into the prehistoric being before it began to dissolve back into the earth. Charlie knew that it could be reborn if anything remained to rebuild itself with after death. Such was the power of this being. *But not this time.*

Charlie stared into the sky. "You, my friends, are at least partly avenged. An eye for an eye, as they say."

His Sasquatch smiled as it thumped back to his side, blood dripping from its face, and misted away into his pouch. "Yeah, I know you're not happy without a little blood sport to keep you in line." He hated doing what he just had to do but he needed answers and his deceased friends needed justice being served. Now the only question remained. *Why are they back? And I hope I don't know the answer already.* But he knew he did.

* * *

"Who was on duty outside the sweat lodge that night?" she asked James. Carol and Charlie had been going over their notes with James in his office.

"Adam McClouskey."

"Call him in and we'll question him in front of you."

When Adam arrived Carol went straight to the point. "Adam, you were on duty the night of the sweat when Ken was killed?"

"Yes." He looked puzzled.

"You reported going back into the lodge. Why was that?"

"Ken, the Elder didn't come out right away so I escorted the prisoners back to the prison door and returned to the sweat to find him."

"And you went back inside the lodge and found him dead."

"Yes. Must have hit his head as he either slipped or was pushed in the panic. It was dark. I checked for a pulse but he had none, then I called the medical staff."

"One further question. Were any of the prisoners in pain? Hurt their hands somehow?"

He looked at her strangely. "Not that I recall."

"Okay thanks. We're done for now. We'll let you know if we need you again." He walked out, looking relieved to be dismissed.

Charlie screwed up his face. "You think he did it?"

Carol closed her eyes. "No, not really, but I think he knows something we don't."

Charlie tapped his cane along the wall as they walked to the canteen. "Don't know, something just isn't right."

James stared at the two. "I'll say this; before you accuse one of my staff you better have your evidence straight. Now get out."

* * *

Carol left to return to the women's side. Charlie kept tapping his cane on the wall by the back doors. *I'm going back to the sweat lodge. Adam, I think, is not our man. I think he's got something to do with it. But not our killer.*

Charlie walked around the inside of the sweat lodge, searching for something; he would only know what when he found it. "Hmm."

As the moonlight shone in and he sat down, he noticed several dark areas and minute punctures, only now visible because of the moonlight. They would not have been evident when he and Carol were in here before. He sniffed the air. *Negative ions. I know what killed our man and caused this damage.*

* * *

Carol walked inside the lodge and crawled back out retracing the steps. “Okay I agree, not bullet holes, similar look with the burned edges but way too small, like damage from highly concentrated lightning blasts or something. Oh, and I’ve checked with medical. None of the inmates were sent off to get medical treatment for burns to their hands. Which leaves me to conclude that someone brought a rock in.”

“And whacked our Elder.”

“A couple of others did report Jan talking to a guard on the way out of the last sweat, which may not have been Adam as, if you remember, Eddie vaguely recalled another one who may or may not have run off. We do know Adam went back to the sweat and found Ken dead so either he also checked for, and removed, any evidence, or the other unidentified guard did before or after Ken was found. The body was left unattended while Adam went for the medics. Whichever it is, I don’t see any discarded rock, just those now laying cold. However it is safe to say that one of the group did murder Ken, we just have to find out which one.”

“Oh, I think we just got kicked off Wardie’s good books.” Charlie grimaced.

“Again,” they both muttered.

“Did I ever mention I hate it when you’re correct?” She put her pen and paper pad back in her pocket.

"I think you've mentioned that a few times. I'm beginning to like this detective business. I should apply to the Vancouver Police Force."

"Yeah, step one, you'd have to get a haircut and ditch the ball cap."

"Nah, I'd get to keep it. Part of my religious beliefs." He winced in pain.

"Religious beliefs, what belief is that? The Blue Jays are going to win the Stanley Cup and that's the second time you've winced. You okay?"

"Yeah, just had an encounter with one of the forest critters, that didn't like chatting much and it's the World Series. You don't watch much sports, do you?"

"I should more often, men running around with taut buns in tight shorts. My kind of viewing. Okay, but you'd still have to get a haircut. And a uniform, before you make detective."

"Think I'll stick to me regular duds and hanging out as your sidekick."

"Sidekick? That ain't going to happen. After this is done I'm going back on holidays and seeing if I could pick up some hunky fireman and have him shag my brains out."

"Carol, my virgin ears just got blistered and burnt. How could you say that?"

"Charlie, some of us have urges besides hanging out with weird forest creatures and inhaling peyote."

"Okay off to see James and get ready to have our ears blasted."

"Again," they both said at the same time.

* * *

Well, the meeting yesterday with James was a bit ugly. But at least he still let Charlie go on his mission with Bryan. Now that I'm stuck here alone and bored let's see if I can find out why our Spritey friend keeps checking me out. Charlie says you're harmless. So, let's see if this works.

Carol set her cell phone camera to video and hit record, then connected up her earbuds. Leaning back against an old cedar tree she inserted the buds and closed her eyes, listening to the sounds being recorded. *Love these cell phones, handy app for a police officer on stake out.* A crack sounded to her left, then her right. The tang of pine or spruce bit her nose. *Farther away, closer, above her. It didn't make any sense, but I suppose spirits do that. No logic, by human standards.*

A hiss of earth. Snake slithering in grass. A trundle of ants marching. A brook babbling away. Lavender and sage flooded the air. Buzz of hummingbirds on flight. A cry of an eagle on patrol. The drone of bees. A mosquito buzzing in her ear. Slithers.

It's testing me, or just curious. She quietly opened her hand and let the glitters from a sparkling brooch catch the light. The half of the handcuff sat open, just above her sleeve.

Oh, you are interested aren't you. The shaman was correct, he said something glittering would catch your attention.

A glint of sunshine in her eyes. A touch on her head, the trembles of spiders running down her arms. Chill like frost touching her brow. A caress of a butterfly's wings. A touch of damp earth, moist. Distracting her as a touch trembled over her palm.

Carol twisted her wrist, the cuff snapped shut. "Gotcha."

Something jerked and Carol opened her eyes. What she could only describe from childhood books as a fairy or a woodland imp glared at her in shock. The face of a creature with green moss as its skin, ferns growing haphazardly on its head, small rows of mushrooms for eyebrows. Dandelions sprouted where ears should be and glistening eyes like dewdrops shone in fear. It smiled and a thud hit her head, before everything went black.

* * *

Charlie wondered if the knocker would come off in his hand as he rapped on the door of the beautiful but very neglected old house. It had needed a new coat of paint, peeling away and a gutter hung forlornly, broken away years ago. Charlie glanced in the backyard over the rickety looking fence. Behind him stood Thomas, Bryan, James and two prison guards.

"Who the fuck is it? If you're selling anything, piss off."

Charlie knocked again, his side still in agony and heavily bandaged from his encounter with the Wasgo. He didn't let Carol know yesterday and almost cancelled, but knew this had to be played out before he met with the sweat group.

"Son of a bitch. If you're Jehovahs you better be off my property before I open this door or you'll be staring at my shotgun." A rustle inside told Charlie he was coming to the door.

Charlie yelled and rang again. "I'm neither."

James barked quietly to his two guards. "Be prepared." They unclicked their holsters and had their hands on the guns that James had thought it necessary they carry today, which wasn't the usual requirement in the prison itself.

The door flung open. "I said piss off." An older man in his sixties stood there. He'd lied about the gun. His face red, his flannel shirt had seen better days and his old jeans needed a washing nearly as bad as Charlie's. His face fell as he stared at the assembled men and guards. Bryan stood behind Griz, out of sight. Charlie knew he was trembling.

"May we come in? This is regarding the matter of Bryan Samuels."

"No. Is the little bastard dead? Good fuc…"

He never got to finish his sentence as Thomas elbowed past Charlie and James, his speed surprising for a man of his size. Although the handcuffs had not been removed he still managed to grab Jimmy by the throat and push him against the far wall. "I really have a thing for bad language. And child abusers." The others rushed in, pictures crashed to the ground. Jimmy gasped as his face began to turn blue. The guards tried to rush by Charlie and James as they all shouldered their way into the narrow entrance.

"Griz, don't kill him yet. We're here for Bryan remember."

"Scum like him shouldn't be allowed to live." He growled loudly.

"If you kill him now, you'll be in jail for a very long time. Now put the gentleman in that chair in the living room and we can do what we came here to do; talk. Otherwise I'll have to shoot you," James yelled out, as the two guards pulled their guns free.

Griz's face snarled. "It ain't worth taking a bullet for slime like you." He let the man go, spitting on him. Jimmy fell to his knees gasping for air, wiping his face.

Charlie realized he needed to finish this quick. He hadn't expected Thomas to be so volatile and he knew if pushed James wouldn't hesitate to give the order to shoot. He could explain a dead convict, wouldn't be able to explain away a dead civilian, even if he should be locked up more than most of those already behind bars.

Jimmy stood and staggered into the living room. The inside of the house was dusty, but otherwise fairly well kept. Charlie grabbed one of the kitchen chairs and set it into the middle of the living room. “Sit. We’ve brought someone along that needs to talk to you.”

He did, still half choking. Thomas moved to the back of the chair. “Get up before he’s done and I’ll brain you, bullet or no.”

James pulled Charlie aside. “This isn’t going how I thought it would. We should leave.”

“And be charged with harassment and entering a building without a search warrant? No, we need to finish this now,” Charlie barked back. He sniffed the air. Something foul, something sickly. The offensive odour was emanating from the old man. “Okay, bring Bryan in.”

The handcuffed man trembled, scratching at himself. “Memories, so many bad memories. I hurt.”

“So this is the house you were in before residential school?”

“Yes.” Charlie hadn’t realized. This could make things difficult. He’d given Bryan some of his potion just before they entered but trying to keep the man focused was going to be difficult.

Surprisingly Bryan lifted his head as he stared at the bewildered man. Recognizing him, his eyes cleared. “Residential School. For most, residential school was hell. For me it was heaven. It kept me away from you. You sick bastard.”

The man tried to get up. Griz thumped him on the head. “Make another move and I’ll break both your legs, gladly, and you won’t be able to try it again.”

The man sat quietly, as if he was awaiting his last rights before being hanged. Maybe he had been half expecting a meeting like this someday. Charlie had read the files and what he did to Bryan was beyond evil. Probably what gave him his split personality, and maybe also his gift.

Bryan walked around the room, unable to stare into the face of the man that had done unspeakable things to him. Still, from somewhere, the resolve came. “He touched me. Bad touch.”

“Son of a …” Thomas growled.

“Thomas, let Bryan speak. He won’t get another chance to ever do this again. Will he Jimmy?”

“No, I’m dying of cancer. Visited the doctor last month, I’ve got a year or so.”

With that Bryan straightened up. The person that had done this would soon be deceased. “I, for one, will be glad for that.”

“Yeah, makes two of us.” Griz backed up the sobbing man.

“He made me sleep naked in the garage, chained up like a dog.” Bryan broke down.

Charlie knew. What horrors people could unleash on each other was at times unspeakable and why? For what purpose?

Bryan answered, as if reading his thoughts. “Bully. You’re nothing but a cowardly bully.”

Charlie closed his eyes. “You, as a young boy. Someone hitting you and …” He hesitated. “Entering you.”

“Yes.” Was all Jimmy could gasp.

“You. You could have stopped this. You could have broken the sickness that was inflicted on you. Instead…”

“Instead, I did what was done to me and worse.” He spat back. “And it felt good. My revenge. Through you. Go ahead, kill me now.”

“I was helpless. I was only a kid.” Bryan sobbed dropping to his knees. “A helpless kid.”

“So was I. Only you were there. A spineless little shit.”

Thomas hammered him on the head again. “Another swear word and you won’t have lips to talk through. Get it?”

"No, it is you that are spineless. You that was a snake. You who could have loved me as the father I never had."

He stood up and walked up to the man. Charlie and James moved forward as well, ready to tackle him if he made a violent move. James motioned to the guards and they held their hands on their guns again.

"Go ahead. Hit me if it makes you feel better. I'm dying anyways. Spit on me, I'm only shit." He stopped. "Worthless."

The beholder stood there wavering.

Charlie walked to stand in front of him and they stared eye to eye. Tears flooding the man's face. So many were screaming inside to strangle the man for what he'd done. "Bryan, come back. Find the words, the one inside that really wants to say what you need to say." Rage tore across his face.

"I know what I'd say before I tore his head off."

"Big Mountain, back off. This is Bryan's moment." Charlie waved him away. Thomas took two steps back. "Now, concentrate. What do you really want to tell this man?" He knew it was now a struggle to keep Bryan intact. He was about to crack wide open and it would be so hard to put him back together.

Bryan reached forward and gently touched the man on the head. "I will never love you. But you were the only parent I ever had or remember." He breathed deep grounding himself. "For that I'm thankful. You aren't worth any more words or efforts. Except for these. I forgive you. For all the sins you committed. I forgive you."

With that he walked out of the house, followed by both guards. James stared wide eyed at Charlie.

Jimmy lifted his face. Tears for the maybe the first time in his life flooded down. "I'm so sorry," he said quietly. Then repeated the words louder so Bryan could hear him.

"Time to go." Charlie said as Jimmy began to sob uncontrollably.

As they closed the door Big Mountain spoke up. "I'd just as soon have broken his neck."

James turned to Charlie. "I don't know what you did back there or how. But that was amazing."

They all began to climb back in the prison van. "I'd call it BOGO. Two for the price of one." Charlie smiled. "And I never had to use my power animals once. Well except for you." He nudged Thomas.

"You, shaman, are quite the person." He nudged Charlie back and sent him flying into the flower bed. Charlie laughed as he spat daisies from his mouth. "You'd make a lousy masseuse. Hell, except if the incredible Hulk had tense back muscles, then I've found our guy." Everyone laughed.

James smiled. "You look good with flowers in your hair. Don't forget your filthy ball cap." Charlie picked it up as he brushed himself off.

Thomas sat beside Bryan, who sat shell-shocked in the van. "You, dude, are okay as well and I want you to join me at my lunch table from now on. We can talk," he said to the man who sat quietly as tears seeped away from him.

James turned to Charlie as they closed the doors to the back. "Again I was wrong. What you did back there was utterly amazing and the scary part, you've no formal training. I think you underestimate yourself; I know you've helped three people today." He nodded back at Thomas who was chatting more to Bryan than he had in the last three months.

"All in a day's work, Boss. That's why you pay me the big bucks. Now I don't know about you, but I've worked up an appetite and I'm really craving smoked salmon and poutine. Nothing like a little greasy dinner before the long ride back."

The two merely snickered to each other as they jumped into the back seats. "Driver, find the nearest - what's the term Charlie used on the way down? – chew-and-choke diner. Dinner's on me."

Chapter Eleven

Her head ached like a bad hangover. Carol blinked and blinked again. She was in utter darkness. *Maybe not so good an idea.* Something beside her moved, pulling her arm slightly. Whatever is was, it was still attached. *Oh yeah.*

She reached for her pocket hoping the cell phone was still there. Her fingers closed on the cubic shape and pulled it free, clicking on the light. Her head pounded like a week-long drinking binge. The wood sprite creature's eyes snapped open. It glared at the cuff in fear, at her, and lurched itself upward flinging Carol into the earthen roof of what must be a cave. Dirt, worms, decomposed leaves and branches rained down on her. Its strength betrayed its diminutive size. It ran along the edges of the cave, causing more muck and debris to rain down on her, dragging Carol along for the ride. *Stop, Shit, Stop*. The cell phone fell to the ground lighting up the entire area causing the imp to freak even more and hurl itself and her back and forth in the room sized cave. "STOP!" she yelled, realizing that was the worst thing she could have done as it grew frantic in trying to loosen itself from her. Carol reached over and flicked the cuffs open as the creature launched itself forward and she fell into the soft ground with a thud. The sprite sped off into the darkness, fading away. "Oh, great. I've set you free and now I'm here, in the dark, in what?"

A very low breathing resounded as she wiped earth and grubs from her face and hair. "Yuck." *What the hell was that?* Under her feet the ground moved like it was alive. She picked up her cell phone and shone it at her feet. *Fuck, been here before*. Memories of finding the dead body of Vancouver's mayor's daughter trapped up inside the old cedar tree and millions of maggots, wood lice and worms cascading down on her returned. Shivers of horror rippled down her spine. The ground moved with millions of grubs. Another slow deep breath. The stench of earthy decay gagged her.

Just when I thought that was the most horrible thing that had ever happened to me. She squinted as she pulled at a worm wiggling down her neck. Ugh. Panic gripped her for a moment.

No. She closed her eyes, breathing deeply. *Calm down, calm down, calm down. Why me? Why not just contact the damned shaman, he'd know what to do. I got to get him to get a cellphone.* Carol laughed to herself. *Who am I kidding. That'll never happen. Although he did learn to use a computer. He's smarter than he looks.*

The slow breathing helped to soothe her as she grabbed the cell phone and with shaking hands shone it around the enclosed area. *He, or it if Charlie is right, ran out of here somehow. Oh, is this is another stunt of Charlie's, I'm gonna shove that cane of his so far up his ass, he'll be wearing Orca for teeth.* Carol grunted, focusing on the light as she moved it about. *Right now it is the only reason I'm getting out of here.*

Only darkness shone back. *Well, how would 'Josephine be nimble' get out of here?* She turned the light back on the floor, two spots of crushed lice glared back. Carol moved forward and spotted another of what she guessed was a disgusting footprint full of crushed bugs, some still flopping in their death throes, and ahead a darkening in the wall. *I ain't eating anything remotely rice-like in the near future. Okay, your exit. Only I don't get the breathing.*

A dark surface told her the exit slanted to the left. Trying to be careful not to crush more bugs than needed Carol inched forward. *Not only rice, nothing with green bits*. Finally a lightness ahead as she inched forward and poked her head into the dim light of a forest. She was a few feet off the ground in the rotted remains of an immense tree. *Trees! Why do I keep getting stuck in a tree. I might take that off my list of favourite things.*

Another low breath and earthy warmth hissed past her. *A living tree? Oh, that's even creepier*. She turned off her phone's light and scrambled out, dropping to the soft cushiony ground of the forest. *Old Spritey must have zapped or teleported us here*. Carol stared around the best she could in the dim light, her eyes becoming a little more accustomed to the gloom. *Yup, dense forest, where though? I could be ten feet away or ten miles and one wrong turn will only take me further away.* Her phone revealed no Wi-Fi or data signal but built in GPS let her know that she wasn't that far from the Penitentiary.

Now, not sure which way to go. Carol stared at the old leather wrist watch she'd worn for years since her dad gave it to her as a graduation present. *How did this work again?* She held the analog watch up against the brightest part of the sky. *It was two when I went for a smoke. Give myself an hour or so.*

She held her watch level and pointed the hour hand at the sun. She knew that the midway point between it and twelve o'clock pointed south and the opposite direction north. *So according to the GPS I'm slightly north and east of the jail. So off I go this way and thanks Dad, didn't think I'd ever have to use my watch like this.*

After about two hours of walking through dense bush Carol came to a clearing. A clear-cut. *Well, makes it easier to travel, but first* she scrambled onto a large stump and rechecked her coordinates with her watch and stared around. *So wonder what happened to ill-o'-the-bloody-wisp.*

Before she got the words out of her mouth a head, or something that looked like a waving bush full of Boston Ferns, popped up from the edge of the clear-cut. "Speak of the green lady herself. You been following me or something?"

The figure stood up and waved her to approach.

Carol slowly began to walk towards the lichen, moss and fern bedecked being. "Why don't you come here where I can see you better?"

The wood sprite stood on the edge and shook its head. Carol stood and stared. "So you can read my mind am I right?"

The fern covered imp nodded back. "But you won't come any closer?"

It nodded affirming her words.

"Why? Unless?" She glanced around. "Is it because I'm standing in a clear-cut?"

It nodded again.

"Now, Charlie did say you weren't bad and even though I tricked and trapped you - I'm sorry for that by the way - I'm not bad either. I think if you can read my thoughts you would already know that."

Another nod.

"So if we are to begin to trust one another, I'm guessing that sticking me in a dark cave wasn't meant to hurt me; or was it?"

The creature's face grew cross.

"Okay, maybe just a knee jerk self-preservation move then?" Carol now stood virtually in front of the peaceful looking being. "I get that you wouldn't harm a flea normally would you?"

A soft sincere smile spread over its face.

"But you won't cross over this boundary will you? I'm curious. What then is it about the clear-cut that is so bad? If I'm to begin to trust you, show me."

The fern creature lifted its hand and as Carol took it into hers the being closed its eyes. A wave of warmth flooded over Carol. She felt the two of them sinking down into the depths of the earth. Carol struggled to stay above ground for a moment. *Okay don't let go and trust.* The earth swallowed them both. *Oh, I just know this is going to involve more bloody grubs and worms.*

* * *

Ebony enclosed everything, as the dank smell of earth wafted. *Yes, grubs coming. I just know it.*

Everything faded away in a sickening spinning sensation, like tumbling into a rabbit's hole and no end in sight.

She slowly awoke into…

Her head throbbed.

Everywhere in front of her dangled…

Roots?

I'm inside the earth?

Her thoughts thick and murky, like thinking underwater.

Like she was a …

Spirit? This feels so odd and weird, what is this…

Carol stared around at the dead remains of roots. Withered like desiccated mummies. She stared closer at the ends and saw what looked like faces frozen in permanent agony. *That's horrible. I get it. Us humans are the worst bad asses with the environment.* The whole area around her was like this with thousands of dead roots screaming in frozen terror. Near the edge she could see the bugs and other little creatures foraging around the edge that the creature stayed back from, unwilling, like her, to enter the horrible zone of death.

Okay I get why you don't like the dead areas of the forest and that it eventually grows back. But why drag me here?

The creature scouted around and eventually picked something up. She held out a tiny blue winged being that looked like a miniature fairy and held it to her mouth pretending to swallow.

You are kidding me? Sorry, I'm not big on snacking on insects. I'll puke if I have to eat that thing.

The creature shook its head. It pretended to swallow the sparkling being and began to move its mouth off like it was reciting a Shakespeare sonnet. Only instead of literature, gibberish and flowers came out of its mouth.

If I swallow this, I will be able to understand you?

It nodded approvingly. Carol took the tiny buzzing creature.

Sorry, little dude, but she told me to eat you. Carol swallowed the being and held her stomach as it immediately began to gurgle away. Finally she burped loudly and a dozen rose petals floated free. Voices and sounds began to filter in; the roots of trees still alive hummed. Below her feet the voices of millions of bugs pestered her for the scraps from her shoes, others cried out as their lives were ending under the crush of her feet.

Hello

Carol jumped backwards as she stared into the face of the Gyhldeptis and heard its voice in her head for the first time.

What you ate is called a communication fairy. It lives off the words coming out of you, like the beings you know as the pilot fish that clean shark's teeth. And in return it lets you hear what other natural living things around you say and think. As she spoke in a singsong voice, petals of flowers erupted and bits of seeds. *You haven't harmed it at all, just let it live its life purpose.*

You've got to be kidding me. Why can't we all get one of these? Would make people think twice about cutting down trees, slapping mosquitos and such if they could hear what I hear.

Very rare and they don't usually take to humans. Can't say why this one wanted to be inside you, but it picked you. This may seem overwhelming at first, but you will learn to control the voices and only hear what is important.

Carol held her hands over her ears. So much input. *Can I get rid of it if I can't control this?*

Just ask it to leave and burp it up. But why would you? It's quite an honour. The Gyhldeptis said in her songlike voice.

Okay, first of all I'm Carol.

Never had name before, didn't matter with our people.

I'm going to call you Glyffy if that's okay? You mean there's more? Charlie just thought there was one of you.

Forest people, people of the forest, how can I be one?

Okay not a trick question.

Now correct me, you're talking without moving your lips.

And so are you. We are in the earth, where we can communicate by thought. Everything that lives here is connected. Travel is easy.

Lives? Underground? But there's nothing here but dirt, roots and probably a lot of grubs. Something whizzed by Carol, a blur. Then another and another.

What was that?

Dwellers, earth spirits, similar to me, others as well. We travel along these lines of earth energy.

So this is like what, a river of spirit. Oh, I think Charlie told me about these.

So, how do I do this, is it like swimming?

The Gyhldeptis read her mind. *No, similar but you move by thinking.* She grabbed her hand. *Like this.*

She pulled them one way then the other, racing past and around great boulders, through underground rivers. Like surf boarding down cascading ocean waves. Glyffy let go and sped off flicking this way and that. Carol fell in pursuit not wanting to get lost, enjoying the thrill of skateboarding under the earth.

The Gyhldeptis spun to the right around a large area. Carol stopped. Coldness not warmth swam before her. The stillness was haunting. Carol swam forward, it was death that greeted her. Nothing moved inside the portion in front of her. Roots all behind her wiggled and hummed. But ahead?

No, I can't go there. It is bad.

Carol entered slowly. She could feel everything behind her, alive and flowing but in this zone stillness. She stared at the roots, hanging limp. Still. Hollow of life. She reached forward and touched one. Screaming entered her head. *Oh God,* she let go and touched another. Searing agony resounded in her. *Christ, this is awful. No wonder Glyffy wouldn't want to come in here.*

Carol lurched herself upwards and stared at a forest of stumps. *This is a clear-cut. Cut of life, only agony and decay lives here.*

Carol closed her eyes and stood back on the edge of the clear-cut. Glyffy stood quietly before her.

Being of the forest and the earth. I'll bet you feel all of those horrors don't you?

I hear still the screams where I go within. So many lives cut. Discon-

nected.

Okay, I get the utter horrors committed here. But if this why you brought me here, I can't help you with this destruction.

No, there is another need. Tears flooded its face as the sun beat down at the edge of the clear-cut.

Why are you interested in me? I didn't think I swallowed a blue fairy so I can discuss environmentalism with some green-headed fern creature.

I cannot enter the contaminated areas by the metal creatures or any metal of unnatural making. You are what are people would call a justifier. I am not allowed to do so.

I kinda got that, you're a creature of nature. Doubt we'd find you in any urban settings.

Cannot enter the unnatural. My world is slowly shrinking.

So the residue left by the saws prevents you from entering? You'd be like a bug put on a counter top.

Worse. I will die if I am cut from the flow of the earth.

Now you said justifier. What do you mean?

Tears welled up in its eyes. *Your people, a Hu-man male committed a most foul act. Trapped and tortured one of my kind. I seek justice and you are capable. I am not.*

Hang on, you contacted me just to get even with someone that committed a crime against your race? I'm a police officer, I attempt to solve crimes and bring perpetrators to justice. I know nothing about arresting someone for violating a fairy being.

You can bring correctness back.

Look I don't think I'm of much help, your ways are bizarre to me. I'm not good at helping others from another species. You've got the wrong chick.

It looked at her perplexed for a moment. *You are not an avian.*

You don't get human sarcasm. It looked at her blankly. *Or even humour of any kind.*

You help the Shaman?

And of course you know him. He travels here underneath. Bloody strange man. Look I'm a police officer. I really don't know how I can do anything for you.

No, you know about the Hu-man ways. I have something about Human that I have to have greatly justified.

Glyffy, with your powers I don't know how you need my help and I've got to learn to be a bastard and say no.

That is why you are a justifier. You can be nothing else. It is in your soul essence. I have a great injustice that plagues my soul and will after you are gone and dead. I live forever, as long as there is natural earth and those that believe in me. As she stood there ferns began to wilt as she shed huge green tears. Moss turned black along her cheeks.

Ah crap, cut that out. I'll do it. Damn, you probably hang out and have coffee with that crazy shaman all the time.

What is coffee?

A hot drink made from a bean that grows on trees native to another part of this world.

You kill plant life and boil its blood to ingest?

Okay, lady, if we're to work together get this straight. I don't know about you, you might live off sunshine and crap out flowers. But I eat salad, green things, cows, little chickens, sushi, yeah raw fishy stuff and fruits. Not to mention drink bovine lactose and wolf down their flesh. I'm on a different part of the food chain. So if we are going to work together, get over it. I can't believe I'm doing this, helping a mad shaman and now some flaky earth sprite. I need my head examined, a stiff glass of Whiskey and a cigarette.

What is whiskey and flaky?

A fermented grain and I hope your blue fairy is not susceptible to lung cancer and can handle tobacco smoking. Yes, we roll up other plants in paper, burn them and inhale the vapours created. As for flaky, read my mind.

A substance of incapacitating qualities made from grains of wheat and addicting inhalations. Why would you? She asked quizzically, unresponsive to Carol's quip about her thoughts of herself.

Lady, be human for a week and I'll bet you'll be chugging the shit back faster than an Irishman at a wake.

I know those of the cloverleaf peoples, they dwell in the ancient lands of the ones you call Leprechauns. I shall trust my decision to engage you in my quest. And I shall stay upwind, so as not to absorb any odours wafting from your pores or foul excrement exiting your body. May my ancestors be with me and guide us in our quest.

Okay lady, lead the way and stay well ahead. Carol reached for one of her cigarettes and lit it.

Hu-mans. So Unnatural.

Fairies, they're so bloody Greenpeace on the save-the-bloody-baby-seals bandwagon.

* * *

Carol followed the Gyhldeptis going deeper into the woods for a few hours along trails established by deer. As far as she could tell they were heading in a northerly direction. Tears ran down the creature's face as they approached a small log cabin set near a river in the middle of nowhere. It trembled, terrified of whatever happened here.

"Wow, that's what I call living off the land and on your own. We're miles from the nearest road." She glanced over at the Gyhldeptis it stood on the edge of a row of tin cans, tears streaming down its face. It slowly let out a slow feral cry like a rabbit in pain howling. *Not a time to be making jokes. What could scare a being that had the powers of this one?*

She kicked aside several of the perimeter of cans set closely together until the Gyhldeptis could walk through them. It did with Carol holding its hand shaking as it crossed the barrier. *I get it, a border of something unnatural to keep spirits like yourself out. But there's more that happened here isn't there? Are you willing to come inside with me?*

I won't enter the building, too horrible for me. Glyffy nodded in return, trembling, eyes brimming over with tears and tiny tadpoles dripping from her face.

Okay, stay here then while I look inside.

Carol entered the unlocked door. "Anyone home?" No response. She walked cautiously around. The fireplace was cold and there wasn't any sign that anyone had been around lately. She walked into a back room and saw several pelts hanging on lines. The stench of decay hung in the air. "That makes sense, he's a trapper. Not a big deal. So why did she bring me here?"

Then Carol saw the gutted skin on the wall, spread like a trophy. A trophy of ferns, moss and, as she approached closer, a face.

My mother. Visions, she knew sent by the Gyhldeptis flooded her head. Caught off guard, pregnant with a baby. She closed her eyes. *With you. Oh god, he cut her open, threw you aside still bleeding and…* Carol sobbed.

Because she was pregnant she had little or no powers to vanish or protect herself.

You ran off as your mother cried out, protecting you, trying to fight him. Only. She sobbed some more. *He slit her throat and, oh God, cut out her tongue, to use as an amulet. It protects him from you and others of your kind. Your mother is his slave, he uses her to hunt other animals. You can't touch him. How could some people be so horribly cruel?*

The visions vanished. A noise from the front of the cabin disturbed her. Everything went dark as the blunt end of a rifle slammed against her head.

Chapter Twelve

"What's going on?" several people asked as they were herded out into the back of the penitentiary grounds.

Charlie counted to make sure all twelve were present. "I've been told by the warden that we're going to perform another sweat with the same group as last time."

Several looked at him in disbelief. "What are you crazy? There's no frigging way I'm going in there again," Jan blurted out.

Charlie waved at the guards that had been assembled outside. "Okay, handcuff those that refuse to enter the sweat lodge and if needed put them into leg irons."

Jan looked hard at the shaman. "You are fucking kidding me?"

Charlie looked hard back, wondering where Carol was, he could sure use her help right about now. "No, I'm not. Refuse and I'll have you in chains and cuffs and if needed gagged. Now get in and we can begin."

She stared harder at him and gave him a slight elbow as she nudged past. He twisted his cane slightly, caught her between the legs. The woman went tumbling down. "What in the …"

"Lady, I dish out what's given. You're playing with someone that's messed with Raven, Sasquatches and more ancient gods than Planters has peanuts and my squirrel buddies tell me they've a shed load of nuts. So we can make this easy or rough. I like the rough stuff."

"Fuck you," was all she could muster, her face turning red with rage as she brushed herself off and entered.

"Love you too, sweetheart." He smiled back. Charlie grabbed Griz and had him hang back as the rest entered the sweat begrudgingly. "Keep an eye on her, I don't trust her," he whispered.

Griz smiled back. "It's okay she's not my idea of dating material."

Charlie was on edge, he smelled a lot of foulness in the air like when he first walked into the sweat lodge and he didn't have Carol here to back him up as fire keeper. The foulness had increased since he'd slain the Wasgo. Someone by now knew what he'd done.

"Okay Billy I'm making you fire keeper. Do you know what has to be done?" He thought he'd pick the one that was least likely involved with what had happened in the last two sweats.

"Works for me. Didn't get much out of the other two. Yeah, I bring in the hot stones when you ask and keep an eye on them out here."

Charlie had the stones heating in the fire for the last couple of hours. As per tradition as each entered he smudged them with sage, sweet grass and cedar. Once everyone was inside, he began to slowly beat on the hide covered drum he'd brought, quietly chanting. He was impressed that everyone, even though nervous about doing this, paid great respect to the ceremony and was quiet. *Unless of course they were crapping themselves with what was about to happen again.* After a few minutes he lit the large pipe he had sitting inside and let everyone inhale from it.

"Okay, Fire Keeper, bring in the bones of mother earth." Which is what Billy did one at a time on a shovel. Some called the rocks grandmothers and grandfathers, Charlie preferred the also-used term 'the bones of mother earth'. Once he'd brought in all seven, the Fire Keeper closed the flap. Only the luminance glow of the fire-red stones lit the darkness. He waited a moment for the stone people spirits in the hot rocks to emerge and mingle around the assembled crowd before he began chanting louder and gave the drum to Griz, who took over in the same tempo as Charlie scooped water from a pail and let the water sizzle and fill the sweat with a hazy mist. Charlie had done many a sweat in his time, mostly by himself.

"As you all know, we consider the sweat to be the most powerful structure on earth. The womb of the earth, its connection to this planet is great." *Maybe why it stirred up the beholder and the others. It probably broke through some sort of mystical plane and alerted the Wasgos. Or at least woke them up.*

A low rumble broke the ground below them. "The connection between the sky, the ground, the four directions all traverse through us and this sweat lodge." Another rumble sounded.

"It's happening again," Griz mumbled to Charlie.

Young Tommy Blackfeathers began to rock back and forth as did Silvia Chartrell.

The sky cracked open again. *I can outside my world. Above me, they sit around smoking rocks. I try to reach up. Only.*

"Bryan, tell me what you see right now."

Bryan muttered into his hands. Charlie had increased the dose of the potion and hoped he could keep him in focus. The man had been a lot calmer since his visit with his uncle. Griz and he had also hung out together a lot, which was good for both of them. "Blackness, snakes frying, lightning and something looking up at us."

"Good. Now before it's too late. As most of you know the former Elder was found dead after the last sweat. You were told it was an accident. Only it wasn't. Ken was murdered. He didn't pass out and fall into the rocks and bash his head. Someone caved his head in with a rock. So it is obvious that our suspect is inside, here amongst us."

Thunder shook the tent as everyone gasped. "At first I suspected some of our more unstable people, like Bryan here, but there's been nothing in the interview or in dealing with him that made me suspect him. Our friend Tommy here is quite out of it." Tommy just rocked back and forth, cringing at every change in the air, every surge of electricity. "Even big Griz, who had quite a chip on his shoulder until I found a way to knock it off. But there is one that sat next to Ken and who after all would suspect a woman?"

"This is a load of shit. I'm out of here," Jan sputtered as she got up.

"Hang on a moment. I didn't say your name, did I Janice? What happened at the last sweat? Or to be more direct, tell me how. Did you smuggle in a rock? Kick it under the loose side of the tent? One that hadn't been heated in the fire, since no signs of burns were on you or anyone else's fingers?"

I am not here in this world alone. I am inside one of them. I... memories began to filter in. I have been led to believe I am alone. I have been deceived.

As another rumble sounding closer broke the air, everyone gasped. A thin vein of electricity surged through the air. Jan, caught off-guard, merely stuttered in reply. "W-what? Are y-you nuts old man?"

"I am. And I thought I'd test a few of you before going for the jugular, but I don't think I have a lot of time before the next thunderstorm hits us and this time I think it's here to stay."

I am not alone. I have been put here to believe I am. I am someone, not human. NO!

The ground vibrated and electricity began to run out from the rocks, tingling everyone.

"We need to get out of here," one of the women yelled. "It's happening again."

"No one leaves until I have my answer. Griz guard the door and pound heads together if needed."

Everyone turned to Jan. "What the fuck is everyone staring at? I didn't…" She cried out as little wormlike beings of electricity began to crawl all over her. "Get them away from me."

The beholder began to cry out. "Electric snakes dancing. Frying the truth from lies."

Tommy slumped forward losing consciousness. His body began to sparkle, sending little bits of electricity over the ground like crawling spiders.

"I am alone. I have been alone for too long," Bryan gasped, scratching at his arms.

Charlie turned to Tommy. His body began to smoulder and tear, like a scene from the Alien movie as something inside was trying to get out. *Damn it! I'd have guessed he was in the beholder.*

I am human only in shell.

Jan moved to pull something from under her prison shirt. Griz moved faster and wrapped his arms around her. "Let go you bastard." She screamed. Charlie reached forward and pulled the thin sliver of metal that looked like a darning needle, about six inches long, from her pocket.

He squinted at the end.

"Hmm, a Shiv. You plan on using this on someone?" Jan growled from a deep heavy voice no one had ever heard before except Charlie. "No choice now. I must kill him before he awakes." Her body began to quiver from under her flesh.

Crap, didn't expect one of those creatures in this group.

"I"

Thunder erupted in the sweat lodge, shaking the ground. From the beach the being that had dwelled alone for most of its long lifetime felt the ocean before him dissolving and behind it a vision of humans inside a sweat lodge began to form around it.

"This is going to get ugly. Hang on," Charlie said as a shadow cracked free from underneath the sweat lodge and a chill filled the area. Coldness seeped into everyone. Frost formed on their faces.

"Silver flakes dance on still breeze," the beholder muttered.

"What the?" One of the women yelled sitting next to him as she felt electricity begin to crawl across her body like worms. She freaked, scratching wildly at herself.

"**AM**."

Lightning tore from Tommy's eyes, erupting upwards, splitting the canvas. "Everyone out!" Charlie yelled as the ground shook again. Tommy sat on his knees, face distorting. Electricity spat from his eyes. Sweat poured down Tommy's face as he grimaced in agony. Lightning began to spew from the back of his head and down his back. Black feathers erupted from his back before a wing flexed free, splitting the shell of what was his arm. The fleshy remains hung limp.

"**THUNDERBIRD**."

The inside of the canvas structure exploded outward in a rush of thunder and lightning. Tommy's body fell away like a rubber shell and on its knees a black, mucousy avian creature emerged. It sat for a moment panting. Wetness oozed down its body and slowly unfurled huge wings over ten feet in length and dangling from each, living lightning that wiggled like snakes. It breathed deeply trying to grasp what had just happened and where it was.

"I am free."

Most everyone scrambled to get away, a couple were unconscious. Others, bleeding and deafened, all were singed like they'd been hit by a massive lightning strike.

"The legends are true. Man, I hate it when I'm right." Charlie, nearly deafened, shook his head trying to get some hearing back as one door from the prison opened and Adam came running into the yard and as he did his body fell away, like a fleshy shell as Tommy's had done. Charlie watched the Wasgo pull itself from the human form as it ran towards them. "Brothers and sisters, kill the shaman, while I deal quickly with Thunderbird before he fully recovers."

Jan and Billy's human forms slipped away as two other Wasgos emerged. Charlie spun around as the two ran at him. "Well, this is an unwelcome surprise."

Chapter Thirteen

When Carol came to her hands and feet were tied and she was perched awkwardly on a low stool.

"I don't get many visitors." The bearded man stood in front of her. He reeked of BO and judging by the smell of his cavity-filled smile he hadn't brushed his teeth, or his long greasy hair, in months, if ever. "And even less attractive female types." He ran his dirty fingers along her shoulders. Carol cringed, already knowing where this was going. She struggled to loosen the knots. His grubby hands ran along the front of her chest and squeezed one of her breasts. Carol glanced around, looking to see if Glyffy was also tied up. She wasn't.

The amulet. Glyffy's thoughts hit her.

"I usually don't have sex with my prey. But in your case I'll make an exception." He smiled evilly. Carol could already see the bulge from his pants. "Now we can make this go easy." He pulled his big hunting knife that, judging by the dried blood stains, he used often, and rubbed the front of his pants. "Or we can make this go hard." He leaned into her and licked the side of her face. "Delicious. I prefer hard myself." He used the same phrase she used on Charlie, which is someone she could really use right about now. Carol closed her eyes and concentrated very hard, calling for him in her head.

He is not available. The shaman with the cane is also in trouble.

Not what she needed to hear. Carol was about to spit in his filthy face when she spotted the thin leather thong tied around his neck dangling free as he leaned into her and what what looked like a piece of dried animal material. Charlie said to her once that's how he holds power over the beings that are his power creatures. *Their tongue.*

YES!

He looked down to slash at the buttons on her uniform. Carol lurched her head forward and clamped her teeth around the dangling tongue. As she ripped it with all of her might from the leather thong around his neck, she brought both legs up hard as she could into his groin.

"What did you do you that for, bitch." He slapped her hard snapping her head to one side. "I was just getting turned on. Now I'm just going to have to cut you up a little first." He grabbed his crotch, doubling over, oblivious to the fact she had the disgusting bit of flesh in her mouth. He slapped her again and she spat blood and the tongue into the corner of the room.

"That's why you bastard." She gasped coughing up more blood. *Glyffy, now would be good.*

* * *

"What the hell is going on? Sounded like a bomb went off in the yard." The warden tried to open the doors to the outside yard.

"I already tried sir. Adam locked them from the outside and he's the only one with the keys," one of the guards replied.

"Damn! Get the battering ram and blow these things open." He could hear thunder cascading, along with screams of rage and panic, from the other side of the door. "I knew I shouldn't have listened to that damned shaman."

* * *

This is trouble. Thunderbird I expected, but not three more of these ancient beings as well. Charlie reached into his medicine bag to release his animal spirits, but before he could the one closest to him leapt into the air, jaws wide, slathering for the taste of the shaman's blood. *It also explains something, the Wasgos, like me, had no idea of who Thunderbird was hiding in.*

A huge beefy fist slammed into the side of the Wasgo's head, sending the creature tumbling away and rendering it unconscious.

"No one touches my shaman," Griz yelled, as he came running up beside Charlie.

The second one leapt at the collapsing remains of Tommy, its mouth opening wide to crush the man's throat in its terrible jaws, hoping to stop the transformation before it was too late. Bryan leapt through the air and slammed aside the beast. "No. Snakes will dance and fry." His own mind wasn't there anymore.

Griz grabbed a hold of either side of its jaws and screamed as his hands dug into teeth and bile. The Wasgo clawed away at the large man, its claws shredding shirt and chest as they struggled. It tried to tear the man's guts open. Blood erupted everywhere. Griz let out a mighty groan. "Ugly bastard, you're pissing me off. I said…" The muscles in his arms tightened and with a massive yank he tore apart the beast's jaws and bent its head backwards.

Crack! The Wasgo's head snapped back at a severe angle and fell away, broken. Blood erupted all over the large native. "Like I said. No one fucks with my shaman."

Thunderbird tried to focus its eyes, shaking cobwebs away. "I, I am Thunderbird." He spoke in an ancient language not heard for thousands of years. "I am not human. Who did this to me?"

"The humans," the Wasgo lied, responding in the same ancient language as it leapt for Thunderbird, trying to catch the great being off guard before it fully awoke. The mythical bird sidestepped its lunge and grabbed it in one claw.

"I think you do not tell the truth." It flicked its wing and zapped the Wasgo with several lightning snakes. Electricity singed in the air, burning the beast. As the Wasgo collapsed, Thunderbird glanced at Charlie. "And you. You are the shaman that entered my domain earlier."

Chapter Fourteen

Mother.

The trapper dove for the flesh Carol had spat out as the door exploded inward and a bizarre deer-like creature appeared. It snorted and stamped on the man's hand as he tried to reach for the tongue. She reached down and, turning the hoof into a hand, picked it up. She inserted it into her mouth.

My daughter can't commit a heinous act. But I don't care and can. I have already been tainted with evil by this horrible person.

The elder Gyhldeptis screamed like a rabbit in agony. It shifted one way and the other as it crossed the room. Long antlers raked across the man's chest. Blood spurted everywhere. Hands transformed into claws she tore into his flesh. He swung the knife blindly at her. Carol closed her eyes to the carnage as decades of pent up rage spewed from the supposedly peaceful being. *I guess even something like Mother Nature can snap, and when it does…*

He screamed and collapsed to the ground, his face torn apart, his chest hanging in shreds. The knife cluttered to the floor. The Gyhldeptis was just a blur spinning around him. Redness splattered left, right, centre as the fairy went into a blinding rage. Claws raked up the back of his legs. He tried to slash at her in vain as he picked up the knife. It almost looked like she was torturing him, in return for all the agony she had gone through. Tendons slashed, he fell forward, unable to stand, the knife clattered to the ground. Still it slashed away at him, shredding man, clothing and flesh.

Carol caught Glyffy keening in the corner, watching everything.

"Stop before it's too late."

The Gyhldeptis stood there its chest heaving. Redness in its eyes receding. Tears flowing down its face, covered in his blood. Carol looked down, she was also drenched in blood, chunks of flesh and clothing.

"Untie me, Glyffy." It did in a couple of quick razor sharp slashes. He moaned in agony, unable to stand up, his tendons dangling loose. The elder Gyhldeptis turned and raised its claws to sink deep into his chest to finish him off. "Stop, you can't kill him."

But he must die now. Not only for what he did to me, but for what my daughter has had to endure all of these years.

"Go ahead, kill me and join me in hell." He gasped, his lips torn to shreds. Glyffy screamed her rage as she surged from the corner.

"Stop! You cannot, he's taunting you."

"Kill me, you bitches."

The elder Gyhldeptis sank to her knees. As the rage left her Carol watched the vegetation adorning its body begin to droop. It had been trapped here too long in an unnatural environment. The transformation had drained most of its lifespan. Browned leaves fell to the ground. *I am dying.*

Glyffy stopped and held her mother's head as she collapsed, fading fast. *Mother.*

Carol stared at the peaceful being trembling in sorrow as her mother died in her arms. "At least you get to hold her one time before she passes this realm."

Glyffy cradled her and hugged her as the elder crumbled away.

"Now, you called me the Justifier. Well here's justice, you can't kill him. That will trigger the wrath of the Sagalie Tyee. But he can die of natural causes." Carol let it scan her mind.

The Gyhldeptis smiled evilly, *I like it, true justice.* Roots sprang from the ground, growing through and over the struggling man. Moments later they walked from the cabin and headed for the river to wash away the blood and matter all over them.

Carol could hear him scream in pain and terror. "Kill me, kill me now. You can't leave me alone with these…" He yelled again.

"I'm so sorry." A horde of horseflies entered the open door to the cabin. Carol knew they'd devour him one small bite at a time in addition to the pile of maggots and larvae the Gyhldeptis had already deposited into the slashed limbs and body cavity. Strong roots were wrapped around his midsection, he wasn't going anywhere.

He screamed again pleading, "Please."

No. Your body will provide a nice home and feeding ground for the next couple of weeks to millions of insects. You will live on becoming food for the earth and the beings you contaminated and tortured, proper fitting torture and justice, for what you did. Only then can your evils be cleansed and your soul saved. The Gyhldeptis dove into the gentle waters of the river beside the cabin. Carol waded in, "Yup sometimes justice is better served slowly than swift retribution." The water around her flowed red with the blood from his body for long moments as she tried to not listen to his screams.

The Glyffy poked its head above the water. *Thank you. I knew you were a justifier. I owe you much and forever am in your debt. I got to hold my mother once before she passed this realm. My heart is in trust with yours.*

Carol strode from the water, the Gyhldeptis simply popped up beside her. She clicked her fingers and a warm breeze swept around Carol, helping to dry her. "Thanks. Now, do you know the way back to the jail?"

Simple. Close your eyes. Carol did and when she opened them she was standing at the edge of the jail grounds. *Man, I wish I had those kind of powers, would save car insurance*. The Gyhldeptis smiled and began to vanish into a mist. *Again, thank you. I am forever in your debt*. It slowly faded, with only its smile remaining, like Alice's Cheshire Cat.

"Man, could I use a smoke. And for once I've got quite the tale to tell Charlie." She pulled the pack of cigarettes from her pocket. Inside were a dozen wet and soggy remains. "Yeah, I guess asking her for some dry tobacco wouldn't be right."

Unnatural whispered around her.

"My thought as well. Okay time to kiss face to the dyke security guard and ask for a favour." Carol brushed herself off. "And see what trouble our Shamanistic friend has got himself into."

Chapter Fifteen

"Griz! Watch out!" Charlie yelled, as the first one shook its head several times, regaining consciousness, one eye swollen nearly shut. It glared at Griz standing over the other dead Wasgo, with its head twisted back at an obscene angle.

"Attack the shaman! Kill him!" yelled the leader. Instead, wanting to avenge the death of its lifetime mate, the beast cried out in rage and ran towards Griz. The native ripped the dangling jaw away and smashed it into the face of the attacking Wasgo as it leapt at him. Griz slammed the jaw into its face, shattering both jaw and face. Bits of bone and fangs flung loose, littering the air as they went down in a tumble. Big Mountain continued trying to mash the fangs into the Wasgo's battered head. A loose fang tore into its other good eye.

Nearly blinded, the Wasgo screamed in pain and rage as they rolled over the grass. "You deal with Thunderbird. This mother is all mine," Griz screamed, as he tore loose a large fang imbedded into the eye of the wolfen beast, blood sputtering free. He shoved it deep into the beast's chest, hitting its heart. It cried out pitifully, going almost instantly limp, life blood cascading over both and the grass. "Die, ugly bastard." Griz hammered away at its face, smashing it into a mess. He continued to yell as his fists hammered at the Wasgo's crushed face, the sound of his own bones cracking under the impact. The whimpering creature fell away and collapsed into a pool of blood and mucus.

Griz stood up, holding his smashed fist. He glared at the other creature, both lay still, obviously dead. Canvas, timbers, bodies, lay broken, and people staggered bewilderingly about.

Thunder exploded and lightning danced over the grounds as Thunderbird lifted skyward. He grabbed Charlie in one set of talons and the Wasgo leader in the other.

The doors to the prison, which Adam had somehow locked, knowing what could be happening in the sweat lodge and not wanting witnessed, blew open as the Warden urged his men outside. They were clutching a police battering ram between them. "What in the hell?" He caught the brief image of the dead Wasgos as they were beginning to dissolve back into the earth.

Griz stared a moment at the two dead Wasgo bodies as they dissolved away. "Charlie! Where's Charlie?" He looked over at the last place he saw Charlie, his cane lay in the grass.

The beholder, one of the few still conscious, merely pointed skyward. "Lonely place, lonely place, goes where the lightning dances." Thunder resounded from above at each flap of a large dark avian shape flying away, lightning flickering from its wings with each sweep, arcing across the sky. Dangling from one talon Charlie hung, from the other a struggling Wasgo. Even with the weight of both, the Thunderbird flew effortlessly away.

The Griz shook him. "Where is that thing taking them?"

He hit his head several times, "Beach, imprisonment, home."

"Tell me and I'll go after him."

The Beholder scratched at his face. "Cannot. His world, not of this world."

One guard lifted his rifle and tried to take aim. The warden put his hand on the muzzle and yanked it down before he could shoot. "Don't! You'll possibly hit the shaman." He stared at the destruction, jagged burn marks radiated out from the remains of the sweat lodge. "I have no idea how I'm going to begin to explain this one in my reports, nor the volume of paperwork I'm going to have to fill out. If anybody gets to shoot that damn native, it'll be me."

Chapter Sixteen

Carol stumbled into the back grounds of the prison. She stared at the exploded remains of the lodge, exhaustion clawing at her lungs. "I gotta give up smoking," she kept gasping.

It looked like a bomb had gone off, thin tendrils of smoke still drifted around. Several of the participants lay moaning on the ground, others staggered about, in obvious shock. All were singed, blackness decorated their faces, prison uniforms were torn. Blood adorned a few. Griz stood in the centre of it all, holding his crumpled hand.

"Good Lord," she yelled as she caught sight of the warden ordering guards about. Carol ran up to him, the centre of what was the lodge now just a burnt out crater with signs of the explosion radiating outwards. "It looks like a bloody bomb went off. What the hell happened?"

"Charlie happened, that's what. I knew I should have not let him do this. Something told me this wasn't going to end well. How am I going to explain it all?"

Seared earth, signs of the concrete prison walls being singed struck her as she looked around. "Yes, it looks like a lightning strike. Where's Charlie? He'd know."

"He's gone."

"What do you mean gone?"

"He went ahead and had the sweat without you. Don't know where you disappeared to. About an hour or so into it, the guards stationed outside along the roof said the inside of the sweat lodge lit up. Then a massive fireball and lightning shot out of it and some kind of big creature, like a black bird, burst forth."

Carol barely heard what he said, "Burst forth? From the sweat lodge? All I want to know is where the hell is Charlie?"

"I said, he's gone. All the others are accounted for, with two dead. Charlie is nowhere to be found."

"Except for this." Griz walked up holding Charlie's sacred Orca-headed cane. He'd looked like he'd gone three rounds with Mohammad Ali sporting razor blade gloves. Blood oozed out of several areas and his one hand hung useless. She could tell the bones in it were broken. "Thunderbird took him and one of the beasts. Flew off."

"Thunderbird?" *The shaman wasn't wrong, there was more going on here than meets the eye, or even the mind.* Carol stood stunned as she took his cane. "I'll hang onto this for safekeeping." Overhead the clouds grumbled as if a storm was approaching. Carol walked around the remains of the lodge, trying to analyze what happened. Two bodies lay with blankets over them. She lifted the sheets, both looked like mere fleshy bags, shrunken beyond belief. "What the..." It was as if they'd been skinned alive and all their insides taken out.

The warden strolled up to her. "I've got reports from some in the lodge that some kind of hairy wolf-like creatures burst from inside these two, along with Adam, and attacked the shaman." He pointed to another bag of flesh cluttered with a prison uniform still on the ground.

"You are kidding me! Well, I ain't got his woo-woo stuff, but this isn't good. He needs my help." She didn't wait for the warden's response but bee-lined it back for the woods where she first met Glyffy. *Damn it, Shaman. As much as I hate to say it, you're right and I'm wrong again, about the woo-woo thing inside someone. Hang on, I'm coming.*

* * *

You shaman, you helped me awake. Coming to my beach with the other mystic.

"What other?"

The dead one.

"The dead one?" In his head Charlie visualized Ken Benson.

It is he. So, why am I here, why have I been alone for so long?

"I do not know. But I know of this."

In his mind Charlie thought of the oral legend he told Sandy's two kids of Thunderbird transformed into a human and…

I forgot, I was made to forget. I thought I was a human. Someone made me forget. Who, shaman, I'm always asking who.

"No, you are an innocent. The Wasgo have done this to you."

Are you truthful?

"Search my memories, search theirs, nothing else will need to be said."

Thunderbird did.

Vile, such vile beasts. They must not go unpunished for such wickedness. I will take you to a place where you cannot escape. In your memories I have parents. What of them? I must seek them.

"Don't know. Legends speak of them going into mountains far away." The mighty bird-god shook Charlie and the Wasgo. Electricity surged through both. Charlie didn't even have time to respond but before he was blasted into unconsciousness, he spotted a sly smile spreading over the Wasgo's face.

Chapter Seventeen

"Glyffy, I know you can hear me. I need your help and I need it now. My friend, the shaman, is in mortal danger."

Carol reverted to talking out loud from habit, but she could still hear Glyffy's responses in her head. As she got to the clearing Carol saw it sitting on a rock. Sunning itself.

You are quick to return.

"I am in dire need, my friend…"

The one with the old cane of wood and crystal is in danger.

"Yes, I know. Can you help me find him?"

I can. But that means becoming one inside the Earth again, only this time it will be harder as you must let go of your humanism.

"I thought as much." She shivered already knowing where this was going.

You do not like bugs. You do not like being in the Earth, my home.

"I know."

You do not...

"Look. Can the holier than thou earth crap. He is in danger and I must help him."

Must like him.

"No, he's a pain in the ass. Drives me crazy. But I know this. If I was in his shoes, he'd come after me, to the ends of the very earth. I cannot do any less for him."

Hmm, I can only believe that for a justifier, honour must be a great meaning. We will go looking. But this will hurt for you and once we begin you must trust me. To go back is death.

"Hurt. Will this be worse than a head full of grubs and wood lice?"

For the first time, Carol watched Glyffy smile and laugh. *I wish I had the Hu-man gift of blundering. This will be much worse even than eating those you mention. Now you need to disentangle yourself from all of the clothen materials entrapping your body.*

Carol gagged. "Naked? I gotta get naked? Charlie, the shit I do for you. And you Glyffy probably mean lying instead of blundering. Okay, now hit me with whatever it is we need to do and get this over with." Carol quickly stripped and folded up all her clothes and slipped them under a bush, along with her badge and gun. She had to do this now or not ever. *Although it makes sense, I guess you can't go gallivanting through the ... whatever she'd call it, the down there, dressed in uniform and revolver. But I sure feel more than naked without some firepower behind me.*

No matter what, you must trust me and stay close. She reached forward and put her hands on each side of Carol's head. *This will be a most difficult journey.*

"Don't suppose I got time for a cigarette?"

The leaves of the tobacco plant will not help with this. Now close your eyes. Carol did and she felt the press of wet Earth and moss-crusted lips. *What the... No wonder she wanted me naked, Charlie this had better work, because I won't dyke it out for anyone else.* Slender fingers of roots erupted from her palms and dug their way into Carol's ears. She screamed as they dug into her brain. A tongue tasting like mud and slime slithered into her mouth. She screamed as the roots tunneled into her mind and the tongue slithered down her throat. Carol gagged, but the Ghyldeptis kept her lips glued to Carol's, holding her with a strength that surprised her. Feeling the wriggling tendrils every movement, Carol fell to her knees.

Yelling as the roots bore their way into her head, her soul, driving down through her neck into the rest of her body.

* * *

Thunderbird's lightning cracked the sky as he entered his former imprisonment. He opened his mighty wings to slow his descent with the weight of the two bodies dragging him down. Charlie fell in a heap to the ground, and moaned, semi awake. As soon as the Wasgo touched the rocky beach his eyes opened and he rose to face the mighty bird. "I'm glad you brought us here to imprison us. Except for one slight problem. You see I put that into your subconscious, realizing a long time ago, that should you awake and escape I'd want you to take me back here." He smiled insidiously.

Charlie, still groggy, lifted his head. *I'm not liking where this is going. Thought that smile on his face meant he was up to something nasty.*

Thunderbird's eyes squinted and thunder broke the air. "What? You admit to being the one that put me here for all of these years?" He screamed in rage, threw one wing back and flung several lightning snakes at the insolent Wasgo. The creature smiled as the snakes sailed limply through the air and bounced off the Wolfen beast. They hit the ground still sizzling, but comatose.

"Ah you see they are asleep. I knew if you ever woke up you might use them against me. And being that this is my realm I created, guess what? They can't harm me." He laughed as the mighty Thunderbird lifted both wings and shook them. The snakes crackled, but all hung limp.

"Oh, and like you I learned something else. I've the ability to transform, only better." He twisted one way and the other as the avian lunged forward to thrust his beak into his heart.

Charlie rose to his knees as the two dueled. *This is no place for a lowly shaman. I need to retreat to somewhere I can think better.* He looked around for his cane, realizing it was back at the jail. *Okay but still got my medicine bag.* Charlie quietly backed up and scrambled for the safety of the forest.

"You see I've also found a way to merge with another as well. It worked well with humans and better I think with arrogant avian gods." In one fell swoop the Wasgo got behind the great bird and grabbed it by the throat. As he opened his mouth to gasp for air the Wasgo changed himself into a fish and dove down the god's throat.

Thunder shuddered across the ground as the bird cried out in anger, before going limp. "Normally you would be too powerful for any of my kind to deal with. That is why we imprisoned you here where we knew we could somewhat control you." Its wings fell limp by its side as its eyes transformed into the Wasgo's. "Ah, yes time again to sleep the sleep of the ages. Amnesia, the humans call it. A wonderful state of mind to be placed in, should someone else enter your head. Ah, forgot to mention another spell I thought of a long time ago." A sly sneer spread over its face. The Thunderbird's sub consciousness faded away as the head of the Wasgo shimmered into view on its body. "Goodnight." He shook the bird's plumage. The snakes awoke crackling and several raced into the air. Lightning exploded across the sky. He glanced around. "Oh, I could get most used to this kind of power." With a thunderous flap of his wings the great bird lifted from the ground.

"Now time to find the Shaman."

Charlie sat against a stone wall. He knew there were old totems near the beach, but this place seemed the best place to defend himself from either of the beasts. He spread out the talismans of the animals he kept inside. Images of martens, the big bear, grey wolf and Sasquatch sprang up. *Well you little fellas aren't going to help me much, not unless he plans to use you to polish his shoes and I know he doesn't wear footwear.*

The sky darkened above him and with a flapping of wings, something thudded on the beach just before him. "You cannot outrun me old man."

"Who's running? I'm waiting for you, right here."

The being he thought was Thunderbird sprang into view as it opened its wings and the head of Wasgo lifted from the body, its evil teeth glinting. It had Thunderbird's body but the clawed paws of the Wasgo. "Most unwise. Do you like my new look?" The mutated being roared.

"You're an abomination. I knew when I caught that sly smile on your face as we were blasted by Thunderbird you had something up your sleeve."

"Hate to explain myself again. Especially when I'm getting hungry. But safe to say I built a couple of failsafe spells in Thunderbird's memory. One to return me to here to deal with or trap me and the other to make it powerless to harm me if it did."

"Very unconventional move. Reminds me of something I'd have thought of. Okay, boys get him." The wolf growled at the black bear and took a swipe at him. "Ah crap, let me guess. Once a wolf…"

"Always a wolf." The Wasgo grimaced, trying to smile. "You, shaman, are mine." The grey wolf leapt on top of the bear and the two tangled themselves into a snarling mess of fangs and claws, tumbling across the grass. Charlie glared at the Sasquatch shuffling nervously behind him and the three martens squatting at its feet. "Okay make me proud." The Martens scrambled forward.

Three lightning snakes blasted them into burnt remains.

The great Bigfoot lurched forward, a loud growl burst its lips. The Wasgo, much faster than the lumbering creature, circled around it, lifting into the air. Lunging in and out, making the great creature look ridiculous as it tore shreds off it and whipped the snakes at it. Blood splattered the ground and singed fur stank the air. It cried in rage unable to lay a paw on the flapping creature. It soon lay in a shredded mess, trembling on the ground. "I have learned from the deaths of my brethren."

The Wasgo leapt over it and thundered towards Charlie. "Now shaman you are done. You are mine."

"Okay, nice to be brave and all. But gotta go." He blew some powder from the palm of his hands that exploded in a horrendous rank cloud in the face of the great beast. A click of Charlie's fingers and the Sasquatch vanished into the confines of his medicine pouch. He would heal him later, if there was a later. The Wasgo fell to the ground gagging and trying to clear his bleary vision.

When he did Charlie was gone.

Chapter Eighteen

Ever have someone reach into your head with their hands, tear out every single molecule that exists of everything you were, every memory, every conscious thought, the very fibre of what makes you an alive human and pull it down into the smallest corporeal entities, then fling it all into down into the rush of cold dank earth, while the throb of living matter invades every fibre, eats it and regurgitate it into the most base of substances known? That which everything subsists on? Dirt and atoms?

Carol fought to keep her sanity and wanted to scream again until her throat was hoarse. Only she had no vocal cords and no throat. She wanted to reach up, to pull herself back out of this environmental insanity. Only she had no arms and no body. It was too late to go back.

Good, you understand, echoed through the darkness. *Now the hard part begins*.

What? Understand what? I have no body. I'm what, just a spirit? Get me the hell out of here.

Welcome to my existence.

A billion burrowing centipedes trod over her. Screaming was beyond her as darkness claimed her serenity and reason hammered her soul to a million icy shards. Falling into a cascade of blossoming crystals and, from the darkness the moon glistened, speaking from its white heart, as felines cried out and hyenas laughed somewhere.

The Gyhldeptis smiled at her as Carol lifted her head, panting. Her mind throbbed worse than the most severe hangover she ever had. She gagged and maggots and wood lice spewed forth. She didn't have to look in the mirror to know she looked like Glyffy. The full moon surged overhead. She wanted to sit and serenade its surreal beauty. *Should I be getting melancholy over the moon?*

Wolves howled, the tread of claws on rock nearby. Glyffy grabbed her. *We need to go before they tear us apart.*

I can't. This is too... She felt the being scanning her thoughts.

We run, unless you want to feel each part of you swallowed and digested into beastly material and processed back into the material we tread on, again. I begin to understand your world, as you begin to understand mine. Or as you would say in your human words, it is now time to dance like bitches in heat.

How'd you know I'd say that? Not responding,

Glyffy grabbed Carol as cackles of crows, howls of bears and the grunt of boars broke the darkness in hunt. They ran arm in arm into the darkness, again. Running for their lives.

On and on, until the two broke into a large glade. Dark trees lined the edges, but only knee high grass, tinged a mellow blue grew within. The Gyhldeptis let go and breathed deep, slumping to the ground. From below bright lights sprang up. Tiny wisps of light began to swirl and rotate around them. Little dancing fairy beings giggled and twisted about. Some kissed her all over. Others sang, their voices sweet as they danced about. *You've made it.*

Made it? To where?

No time to explain, we must hurry, your shaman is in grave danger. We have other spirits we must call upon to help him.

Where? Carol didn't have to ask, she knew as soon as she did. She was part of the earth, she was the earth. Connected. With that they vanished, like water dissolving into the ground, the two swimming along the magnetic waves of energy. *This feels bloody amazing, and she was right, way better than a cigarette.*

* * *

Charlie pulled his small switchblade from his jeans' pocket and stabbed it into the totem with the three watchmen. Behind him on the beach several ancient totems stood, some fallen onto the sandy shores. Others at obscure angles, waiting for the next storm or winds to send them crashing to the earth. "It is here I make my stand."

He didn't know how this world was connected to the others or if he was on earth somewhere, just in some sort of spell protected area. He hoped the latter. He flung off his jean jacket and tossed his ball cap aside, unbraiding his hair. The shaman rolled up his sleeves and sat down legs crossed under him. "If you are hearing me spirits, I'm pleading here. I've run out of options." His power animals defeated, it was up to him to prepare to die with dignity.

He heard the heavy crunch of the Wasgo's paws, the gasp from the blowhole above its shoulders, the crackling flap of the black wings, air sizzling. Charlie stood up and yanked the blade from the tree. Strangely a small amount of sap oozed down from the long dead tree. *Okay, something is listening.*

The Wasgo approached slowly. "I would prefer to hunt down my prey."

"Yeah, well I prefer to die like a warrior. You forget, I've Haida warrior blood in my veins."

"And you forget, I'm a merciless killer. And fresh meat is fresh meat."

It lunged at the shaman. Charlie sidestepped the attack and stabbed down into the shoulder of the creature. The beast screamed in rage. It swatted Charlie aside, sending him flying. The creature closed its eyes and transformed itself into a more human form and reached behind itself, disjointing its arm in order to pull out the offending knife.

Charlie lifted his hands as it flung several lightning snakes at him. One snake hit both hands and electricity blasted the shaman. His hands were blackened. The Wasgo leaped on top of him as Charlie collapsed to the ground. But he couldn't match the strength of the beast with numb hands as it stabbed down and punctured his chest just below the heart with his own knife.

The Wasgo, knowing he had him, now smiled, its fetid breath washing over Charlie. "Ah, you see. I know of your love as well."

"What, Lucy?" *How could he?* The shaman winced in pain as his blood erupted from his chest.

"Yes, and I have sealed her away in a place you'll never find her."

"How?" Even though she was dead, he knew she dwelled along the shores of the river that crosses the realms of life and death waiting for him. Pain creased his face. He had to think. *A way out. Time, so hard to think, need time.*

"For I not only planted the memories in Bryan of the Thunderbird, but the writing as well."

"That wasn't Thunderbird?" No wonder he had got the feeling of evil and darkness every time he was in that cell. *I was foolish, I smelled something wrong, but couldn't place it.*

"No, I could read Bryan's mind through his powers after I awoke and learned of you and your love, Lucy. But I couldn't find the human Thunderbird was trapped in."

"You used Bryan. Vile beast."

"Most wonderful when a plan comes to fruition. I owe you a debt of gratitude for helping me find Thunderbird, a debt I won't be able to repay. Well, except for letting you become my next meal. You are a courageous and strong opponent, I shall enjoy adding your cunning to my essence." He knew that if a warrior defeated another, he could absorb his strengths as well.

Charlie closed his eyes. He was about to die.

From the darkness of the forest a rhythmic breeze stirred like breathing. It surged closer, closing in on the two on the ground.

A gasp from the still breath of the watchmen looking down from their places atop the old fading totem poles echoed.

Calling.

Charlie listened, his ears ringing to the haunting whispers treading the woods. "Do you hear that?"

"No! Shaman, stalling your death ain't going to help you. But why should I finish you off so quick? Like the forest-bound cats, I sometimes like to play with my food before I devour it. In any case, you, shaman, are beaten and destroyed." He flinched the knife blade slightly and Charlie cried out in agony, his blood sputtering free, oozing down his back onto the ground. From below he felt something lick at the moist blood. Hee tried to hold the knife from penetrating further, but his strength was fading.

"Such a sucker for punishment. You ain't hearing then what I am. Whistling through the totems. Ancient whispers. The old voices are gathering."

The Wasgo lifted its head, straining to listen and sniffed deeply. "I sense nothing. You forget this is my realm, everything here I created.

You're messed old man, but go ahead and babble while I watch you suffer." He flinched the blade again, more blood oozed out.

Charlie moaned. If he moved the blade a centimeter up, it would pierce his heart. "We're not alone."

Rhythmic breezes wrapped themselves around the ancient monuments, pulling mist from the old carved figures. Remembrances of… once being … stirred.

"There is no one here, demented shaman, you are doomed, finished, get it?" The gloating Wasgo snarled.

"Ah, I do beg your pardon, but a good man travels with friends, while the likes of your ilk usually travel alone," the Shaman gasped.

"What do you talk about?" The Wasgo glared at him as the truth stung at him. He was alone, except when he hunted for a mate and that was just to perpetuate the species.

"It's obvious you don't trust others to help you and sometimes I think not even yourself. Kinda of like having to always look over your shoulder, waiting for the hidden knife to thrust at you." Charlie groaned, not knowing how long he could hang on as the blade moved up slightly.

"The only knife doing any thrusting is this one into your heart." The being hesitated and held the blade into the shaman's chest. "I don't need others. I have my power, my fear to keep the others in line."

Charlie smiled through the pain searing his chest, sweat pouring down his face. "If I can interrupt, much is to be said about a man admired by those around him. That they …"

From the wood visions of mist poured forth, blurring the air as beings long cast into the forgotten history of wood breathed back into being. A deep growl rent the air.

The creature lifted its head. "What?"

He watched the creatures as mythical as itself, only carved by hands so long dead, shake themselves from the encumbrances of cedar. Pulling rotted wood free, turning into beings of corporality. Three squat Watchmen crawled down the beings piled high on the totem.

"It is not possible."

Wolf smouldered, Bear growled as Eagle thrust its wings skyward, pulling themselves free from the wooden forms they'd been carved into. "No, it is too late for you Ska-ga. They will not save you." He thrust downwards.

Charlie screamed and grabbed the hilt of the knife, crying out as intense pain seared through him. From the earth where his blood had seeped a hand shaped like a root reached up beside him. Grabbing the sharp edge of the knife, it began to push up. "Yeah, I don't think so. My ancestors have answered my cries."

The Wasgo warped between the Thunderbird and his true fish, serpent-like form. Charlie's fingers dug into the fishy talons. The Wasgo leaned into the blade, knowing it had to end now. Smoke poured into the shaman, into his heart and arm. His wolf and bear and others of the totems crept towards the creature. From underneath the shaman white energy surged into him, reenergizing him, sealing the wound.

We have come.

"What? This is not possible." It tried to push down harder, unable.

Charlie grasped the knife with one hand and whatever was below him with its root-like appendage, also did. The blade shook under the intense contest of wills and strength, until slowly the knife was pulled upward from him. The Wasgo screamed in rage, redoubling his efforts. The blade stopped and slowly descended again.

"No-o. Not possible," it cried, having to defend itself as the spirit

Bear and Beaver jumped on its back. It had to use one arm to swat them aside, flinging electrified snakes. Air stank, ripe with thunder and charred flesh and incinerated wood.

With the Wasgo distracted, Charlie crushed the talons under his fingers. Wasgo cried in agony, feeling true pain for the first time in centuries. Charlie's knife fell free to the earth as his gaping wound sealed itself and flooded the shaman with white energies from below.

From the shadows an old black form moved. Answering the call like the others, it resolved not to help the shaman, perhaps hoping he would die this day, instead. Long black wings wrapped around itself. "Stinkwaters, another day." It absorbed itself back into the earth, knowing it could not win this battle if it chose to engage the shaman.

Charlie slammed his one hand into the Wasgo's/Thunderbird's chest as it screamed rage at the Watchmen with long teeth, gnawing on his legs. As it lifted itself to fly skyward, Charlie tore from its chest a beating heart, hot blood cascading down. Gasping, the Wasgo tumbled to the ground as Charlie stepped aside.

"No-o-o." It screamed, failing to capture its breath. "How? You've… you've…beaten me."

Smoke poured into the being's heart thumping in the Shaman's fingers, as blood poured down his arm. With his other free arm Charlie thrust again into the beast's chest and pulled free a second heart. "Don't ever mess with me again." The Wasgo slumped onto its knees, skin turning blue.

The shaman thought hard as he poured the magic of the ancient dwellers into the second heart while the Wasgo gagged for breath. Charlie cupped it in his hand, whispered a few words, whistled his breath over it and flung it free.

Quickly transforming into a sparrow it beat its wings, lifting skyward. Another beat and it mottled into an eagle. Thunder crashed across the sky and as it changed again, the massive black wings of Thunderbird thumped the air. Electric snakes sizzled, arcing lightning across the sky. "My thanks Shaman. I'm off to seek my parents." With that the massive bird exploded in a blinding blast and vanished.

Charlie stared at the gasping Wasgo, now stripped of anything to do with Thunderbird. He held the other heart watching its beats slowly fade. The Wasgo's eyes tilted back, paws fell away limp and he fell to one side. Glancing at the heart and back at the dying god, his heart cooling in his fingers. Charlie concentrated hard, whispered again, poured white misty breath over the nearly still heart and slammed it back into the vile creature. The earth's mists poured up into the cavity, healing the massive gaping hole.

He knew the beast spoke the truth. Lucy would be gone when he went to search for her and his life would remain empty forever until he found her again. He patted the healing chest of the Wolfen beast. "Everything that you ever loved, taken away, I give back to you. Think about that with every breath you draw after today."

The heart thumped with renewed vigor as it reconnected, the wood spirits flowing strongly around the barely living creature. Life began to flow back into his veins, colour returning to the fierce face. Coughing up mucus, he groaned, "Why?" The mighty beast shuddered as coldness washed away. "Why do I not die this day?"

He stared into Charlie's eyes. "You've…Saved me? I don't understand."

"Can the thanks. Just send me roses someday and the odd twenty, helps pay the cable bill for those baseball games." Charlie stood up. "Oh, and just a little teensy, weensy problem with letting you live."

"Why did you?" He looked at his paws that had done so many terrible things.

"Because I'm not you." The shaman slowly walked away. "Consider that my repayment."

The Wasgo sat up on its his knees. "You bastard," it gasped. Realizing. Eyes welled up. "And I've been so nasty, so vile."

For the first time in its life, tears flooded its face. "I'm not me. You've given me a real heart, my heart. You've changed me."

"Yeah, I reckon you've a got a few dozen diaries to write about the lifetimes you could have been just, you know, a decent fish/wolf/serpent type being." Charlie walked up to the crumbling totems as the Wasgo sank its crying face into its paws.

The beings in the mists swirled about, fading away back into the confines of the forest. Charlie stared at the being slowly being reabsorbed back into the ancient woods of the old corroding totems. Faces stiffening, eyes cpening into avoid stares. "My humblest thanks for saving me. I know you can't answer and I haven't the foggiest idea how you did this, but thanks. Detective." He watched as toothy grimaces filled the faces of the watchmen who just returned to staring out at the ocean before them. "Haw-aa. Thank you." One of the watchmen slowly winked back.

The Wasgo slunk towards the beach, its deep sobs echoing into the air.

"I must go, I really hate cry babies." Charlie grabbed a rock and walloped himself on the head, returning to his world.

How is it you can feel like you've won the war, but still feel empty inside?

Chapter Nineteen

Carol pulled herself back up into the glade where she first met the Ghyldeptis at the back of the prison. *You did say I could return to my former self.*

Yes, but I thought you'd like to stay with me.

Thanks, but no thanks. Not that you're not beautiful, it's just a woman with ferns and slugs in her hair isn't really my game. I'm usually attracted to beings with harder sticks between their legs. Now, what slimy bug infested hell do I have to go through to return? Carol was expecting the same sort of hell she went through to get into this earth-connected state, but hoped it didn't entail another long kiss from her. Giggling, she pulled a large centipede through her mossy hair and shivered as she tossed it aside. *A mother of a long shower is first on the agenda, with a damn lot of soap.*

Glyffy pulled a small orange slug from her hair. She whispered something to it and the bug began to glow and sparkle. *Swallow this quick.*

You are kidding me! You want me to swallow that? Carol gagged.

It is the only way. But the effects I've instilled are only short term, you must swallow it quick before the creature dies. I haven't the energy to do this twice before the full moon.

Crap. She grabbed the slug and chucked it down her throat, swallowing several times, and trying very hard not to puke it back up. Almost immediately the ferns adorning her body began to wither and the insects infecting it and other parts of her body fell away, scattering back into the earth. *Although you could have asked for my advice. I'd have gladly taken one of these horribly disgusting things, instead of all that mind-altering root jamming my brain cells. Oh, and not to mention the swabbing the back of my lungs with that incredibly long tongue of yours. Although I know of some ladies back in the pen that would appreciate that. A lot.*

It is, as you Hu-mans call, like preparing two hours for a great meal and spending five minutes devouring it. If too easy you would not appreciate it and I rather enjoyed the process.

Carol felt the wonderful sensations of earth connection filtering away. The exquisite sounds of roots humming and the singing of the larvae waiting to be born faded. Like taking a shower in reverse she felt herself being sprayed upwards. The particles as they fell reorganized themselves back into flesh and blood. She felt herself trembling as the pleasant sensations of a complete gentle body orgasm shook her to her core and she soon stood there stark naked again. Her voice returned to normal from the soft mystical tones reverberating with the earth's sighs. "Oh man! That was quite the trip."

Glyffy never took her eyes off her body. "I'm glad to be back to normal. Although I think I'll miss some of that woo-woo stuff. Could I ever do that again?" She moved around, letting the being get an eyeful, not knowing if that was part of the reformation or something the fairy being had done to her, making her feel rather sensuous inside.

No, that is only a once in a lifetime journey. A second time and you would remain as me. Although you did look more attractive before. Ferns look rather erotic on you.

"Ah, look lady, we had a great time together. But like I said not my type. I prefer…"

More testosterone based creatures. I understand. But it is not just Humans that are attracted to the same species.

"Sex. You mean same sex."

Yes. Now I must go. With that Ghyldeptis dissolved into the ground as tears of sadness cascaded down its face. On the light scattering of the winds whispered, *Again Thank you for helping me*, fading into the background.

"Look, sorry about not being the right type thing. But again thank you very much for saving my friend. I don't suppose we could ever get together for a coffee," Carol said to the cool air around her as she moved to get her clothes and there, on top of the pile, lay a single red rose. "Let me guess, she doesn't ingest leaves of the coffee tree. Might explain why she came to me instead of Charlie." Carol dressed quickly. *Although it's still men in particular and large hotdogs in general.*

* * *

James walked into Charlie's office. "Excuse me, but I hear from the inmates and the guards that a lot of the drug supply has dried up suddenly."

"Oh really? Most odd that." Charlie looked up from under his ball cap. "Probably something to do with the El Nino winds or some such nonsense."

"Yes, most odd. One of my guards mentioned a conversation you had with him a while ago. Would you know anything about this?"

"Hey James, I'm just the Elder around here. My job is to keep the natives in line and happy with their buffalo ancestors, perform sweats and give them hope. What do I know of drug smugglers?"

"Hmm, nothing to do with reports of large hairy beasts patrolling the woods just outside our borders?"

"Hey boss man I've only seen a Sasquatch in my nightmares. Quite big, scary and smelly. That musk thing they got going on may attract other Sasquatches but little else."

James turned and opened the door to Charlie's office. "Thought you had something to do with it. I will say thanks, however you managed to pull that off. Don't care, don't want to know. But thanks again. Now I believe we have a Florence Sanderson just arrived and Griz, er Thomas - man, now you've got me calling him that - is out back ready to meet her." He walked out.

Charlie thought a moment. *Tricky bugger. He never said what kind of beast it was. Caught me out. I guess that's why they pay him the big bucks*.

As Charlie entered the courtyard Griz stood pacing beside the now rebuilt sweat lodge. Two armed guards watched, the warden's call. Although he needn't have bothered. Thomas was nervous. For all of his anger and hate, Charlie knew the man was in a place he never thought he'd be and he didn't know what to do with it. "How'd you arrange a meeting out here in the back of the pen?" Griz asked.

"Well, after saving my life - although I think he would have preferred it if the Wasgos ate me - I talked to the warden and he agreed. I know you wouldn't make a break for it and you'd be more comfortable here than in a room. Not only that, but he has given me the privilege of letting you know he's awarding a full pardon, for helping save the lives of all involved in the Sweat lodge and the handling of Bryan. If it wasn't for you I'd most likely be fish food right about now. So after you've spent enough time with your mom, you're free to pack up and leave with her for good. And no coming back, or I'll just have to kick your scrawny ass."

Thomas laughed at Charlie. "Shaman, any time you think you're tough enough, bring a couple of those power animal dudes of yours and

I'll tie a hand behind my back. Could be a fair fight then. But sincerely, I've never said this to anyone, ever before." He reached his hand out. "Thank you."

Even though Griz still sported several bandages and a splint on his left hand, Charlie still felt the strength in his handshake, but this time the intimidation was gone and the handshake was firm and gentle at the same time. The door to the yard opened and an older lady Charlie recognized as Florence Sanderson walked into the light. Attired in a floral dress, her hair up in a bun. She looked elegant, but that façade ended as Thomas turned and saw her. "Mom?"

"Thomas. Oh God!" She dropped her large handbag and ran full tilt for the son she had never seen before today other than as a toddler. Thomas took two steps forward and dropped to his knees in order to hug the smaller lady. Both burst into tears, crying uncontrollably. Charlie hoped that by having no one around Griz could let everything inside that he'd been holding, go. As he sobbed huge tears and his mother hugged him, caressing his head and kissing his cheek, he knew he'd made the right move.

Charlie walked back to the two guards. "Yup, I guess this job has some pretty good fringe benefits after all." He wiped at a tear on his cheek.

"You okay, old man?" asked one of the guards.

"Yup, just got something in my eye." He walked away as mother and son talked in the yard. Thomas lifted his shirt sleeve and showed his mother the birthmark. They sobbed their eyes out and hugged for a long time.

Epilogue

Charlie sat across from Carol at the restaurant. Carol had finished working at the penitentiary the day before and had decided to have lunch with Charlie before she left. "I'm going to stick around until the end of the month. The warden tells me they've a serious problem with some nasty rodents and annoying squirrels out back."

"Let me guess. You can talk to these pesky creatures on a personal basis?" *He'll never change will he?*

"Mano on mano. So did you know that the Buddhists not only believe in re-incarnation, but they also believe that not only are we reborn in another lifetime, we are sometimes here in different lifetimes, at the same time."

"Wow, that's messed up and trippy thinking. Probably invented by some high powered brain guys like Einstein tripping out on Mary Jane. So you're saying I could bump into my future self?" Carol responded.

"Or the other way around, past self. This is why sometimes you run into someone and feel like you already know them."

"Because I already do?"

"Because they are you, were you or will become you!"

"Charlie I don't know what you smoke or put into your teapot in that cabin you live in all by yourself but that is twisted." *Man, does he read a lot or at least watch too much educational TV. My depth of mysticism is lighting candles and the odd incense cone before a bath with some hunky male. With the plan to get him deep into me and not me into my head.*

"Did the Ghyldeptis not feel familiar? Most people would be freaked out seeing her. In fact from my experience most people can't see her, just familiars. She is a future reincarnation of you. I felt that when you were rescuing me. There was the spirit of two Carols there. And how do you think she knew to come to you to seek justice?" He smiled at her.

"Yeah, here let me unbraid your hair. I think you've wound them too tight again. I thought we'd have a pleasant teary-eyed last meeting before I left. Man, you always surprise me with what comes out of the mouth." She shook her head. *Too bad they couldn't add a little whiskey to my coffee.*

"Man, it didn't take me long after we first met to realize that you, Charlie Stillwaters, are a pretty deep thinker for a guy that just sits out in the woods and chats to squirrels." Carol took a deep slug of her coffee.

"And robins and martens."

She snickered. "Yes, can't forget about those. So what you're saying is in the future I turn into her."

"Yes. Did she not say that the effects of the transformation slug were only temporary? From my understanding of that line of spirits, they can be a bit tricky and if one has transformed the effects can't be reversed forever."

"I guess. And I'll like girls eventually? Yuk. Better get my fill of men while I can then." They both laughed. Carol had told Charlie that she tried hitting on her after the rescue. "But I did want to show you this headline I read before you showed up."

'Unprecedented Salmon Run entering the Fraser River. Largest since 1915'.

"Well, I'll be. Maybe there's hope in this world yet. I told you legends say that when Thunderbird returns so do the salmon. He was their protector."

"Yeah lucky coincidence." Carol stared up at him, "I've booked the last week of my holiday over in Hawaii. No Thunderbirds, sea spirits, or

Gyhldeptis. Speaking of Thunderbird, you going after him or worried he's coming after you?"

"Not really. I set him free so I don't think he'll be back, and unlike he-who-should-not-be-named, the dude that keeps bumping into me on shopping trips. Man, I gotta switch to online shopping, meet less freak jobs that way. Thunderbird is basically a good being. He's a little bit cranky about being trapped in human form and being tormented by the people in the residential programs. He's more apt to raise some nasty thunderstorms or seek revenge on a few former teachers. But overall I think I'm safe. Besides I did get something from the dead skin of Tommy Blackfeathers while he was in the morgue after I came back. Call it insurance."

Carol thought for a moment. "Gross. You are not telling me you've got a piece of a man's tongue inside that medicine bag."

"Are you asking?" He looked at her blankly.

"Ah. No. Don't want to have to arrest you for concealing or the transportation of human body parts." *Some things were better left unsaid.* Besides he did save her life more than once. Not to mention he got her in a shed load of trouble and nearly got killed several times over it.

"Actually I put into its sub conscious the thought that as it flew away it would forget ever meeting me or the Wasgo."

"And this wascally thing is, how shall I put it, behind bars?"

"It's Wasgo, emphasis on the W."

Carol shook her head. "Nah, you got a piece of that man's tongue in your bag. I'm not a sucker for a fast one, Charlie Stillwaters." She thought a moment. "So hang on, let me back up a moment here. You saying that by me meeting you here at this prison, I will become Glyffy in the future? And if I didn't meet you I never would become her?"

"Correct. You are the sum total of everything you've done in your life up 'til now and every action produces a result. Some cultures also believe that there are alternative timelines running as well as others. The real question you need to ask is, why did that being contact you and not me when I had the more woo-woo experience to deal with whatever she needed handling? There is a reason. By the way, what did she want help with?"

She shivered, remembering the trapper's vile hands touching her. "I swore to her that I'd never tell anyone. And that I'd like girls not in this lifetime, Shaman." She stared hard at him. "You, Mister Woo-woo you probably already know why." *While I didn't kill the trapper, I should have reported his death. Only how could I explain to the authorities that a spirit being attacked him? They'd lock me up longer than Charles Manson.*

"I've got a few ideas."

"Let me guess, you ain't telling?"

"Well that would wreck the climax wouldn't it?"

Carol threw her arms up in the air. "I think talking to the stone walls of that prison got me more sense. Why do I bother, except to irritate myself beyond belief?"

"Cause you know I'm most curious and smart with total understanding of FIOAT, the fundamental interconnectedness of all things."

"And my gun's butt I wish sometimes." Carol played out the first letters in her head. *He really watches too much TV. Needs a woman in his life. Only who'd be crazy enough to…?*

"So remember this, it explains FIOAT quite well. If a moth farts in Bolivia, why does it cause a gorilla to scratch its butt in the Congo?"

Carol stared blinking, recalling the old cliché 'if a butterfly beats its wings, hurricanes form over Texas'. "First of all moths don't fart."

"Ah, just because you never heard one, doesn't mean they don't. The old 'if a tree falls in the forest and no one is around to hear it' philosophy."

"This is complete and utter BS. Time to say goodbye, shaman."

"Besides, bullshit has more connection with melting of the ice caps. Global warming from all the methane gases and such." He smiled at her from under his ball cap.

She stared hard at the man that as long as she knew him, she'd probably never truly understand him. "Some days I really would like to see inside that noggin of yours and then I grab a smoke and a strong coffee and think to myself I'm better off not knowing what clanks and bangs around in there. That's a pretty scary view of life you've got. All I know I've been given an extra week off due to solving this case and I ain't spending it anywhere around this prison. Although I will say thanks for the adventure, it's not every day I can travel the ley lines, have women want to either deep tongue me or put a knife into my guts and meet some bizarre creatures that I'd normally only read about in some Harry Potter type book."

"Looks like you owe me another favour."

"Favour? Crap, this is beginning to be a habit, like some sort of ongoing TV series or book deal."

Charlie closed one eye for a moment, in thought. "Oh, I don't know, Stillwaters and Ainsworth Detective agency has quite a ring to it. Fifty-fifty split, could work."

"Ainsworth/Stillwaters has a better ring to it. seventy-thirty. Can't believe I'm saying this. Look no offence, but if I don't get some private time, on a beach, mai-tai in my hand and maybe a hunky ex fireman to shag my brains out, I'm going to go stir crazy. I've seen enough heebee geebee's to last a lifetime."

He continued, obviously ignoring her. "Or we could call it CCC Detective Agency. Our slogan could be Charlie and Carol, 'We C it all." He laughed. "We could put a little eye logo underneath."

He drew a picture of an eyeball with Charlie and Carol written over the top and 'we see it all' underneath.

"Change my mind, since I'm officially back on my holidays, the only thing I'm going to C is myself off to a stiff drink and something else with a stiff C in it." Carol uttered, "Hey, waitress! A double whiskey stiff, one ice cube and no other rocks."

"Yeah could use a drink myself. Beer, heavy on the root and plenty of ice."

"Now, you're talking. But it was one hell of a crazy time. I will admit beats stake out over a crime scene, which is probably what all I'll be doing when I get back."

"See, working with a bona-fide shaman ain't so bad after all. Great fringe benefits."

"Like what being put in a prison full of women that just want to wrap their lips around mine? Or pulling grubs out of my ears, butt and other orifices. What did I ever do wrong in a past lifetime?" She squirmed remembering all the maggots and wood lice crawling over her.

"Ah, I could find out for you." He softly smiled.

Carol stared at him as she downed her drink in one go and flagged the waitress. "I'll have another one of these." Carol glared at him. "That is exactly the problem, you probably could find out. Man, you're one weird dude, Charlie Stillwaters."

"Yeah, some of us weren't made in moulds at all."

Epilogue (Post Credit)

Charlie glanced at Carol. “Why have they got you wearing a uniform on the cover of the book?”

“Uniforms sell better, viewer recognition and all. Besides I think it makes me look hot. Why are you wearing that wild Thunderbird outfit?”

Charlie scrunched his face. “Nobody could find a Montreal Expos ball cap and I think it makes me looks native chic.”

“Think it makes you look hot?”

“No, just hot. I sweat like a badger under hides. Don’t know how the old natives did it.”

“I reckon they didn’t wear underwear.” Carol surmised.

“Hey, who says I do.”

“Eew, gross.” She laughed.

About the Author

Frank Talaber was born in Beaverlodge, Alberta, where the claim to fame is a fox with flashing eyes in the only pub. Yeah, big place, that's why his family left when he was knee-high to a grasshopper and moved to Edmonton, Alberta. Eventually he grew tired of ten months of winter and two months of bad slush and moved to Chilliwack, BC. Great place: cedar trees, can cut the grass nine months of the year and, oh, it does snow here once or twice. Just enough to have to find out what happened to the snow shovel and have to use it.

He's spent most of his life either fixing cars or managing automotive shops, and at sixty is blessed with two children (okay, he had them earlier and they've grown up and begun living on their own) and a bonkers-mad English wife. His insatiable zest for life, the environment, and the little muses that keep twigging on his pencil won't let his writing pad stay blank.

Over the years he's had multiple short stories published, been short-listed in contests, written several blogs and had a few automotive articles published in RV magazines. Currently he has five novels published. And five others to be released.

When asked, "Where does this creativity spring from?" he answers, "From the Gypsy blood in my mother's Hungarian ancestry." His literary madness drives his wife crazy when he leaves their bed in the middle of the night to jot down another episode of muse-induced brilliance. "Here we go again, the next War and Peace, 21st century," she moans, only to realize there's no lead in his pencil and he's scribbled on sixteen blank pages in the dark.

He can usually be found puttering around the yard of their heritage home, talking inanely to the squirrels or wondering how one can plant a dozen flower seeds and get five thousand weeds. His habit is to wake early in the morning to write, when it's just the pencil, his imagination, and the raccoons that wander by looking for handouts. He makes some amazing home-brewed wine, as most guests will confirm as they stagger out the door.

A Writer by Soul.

A natural storyteller, whose compelling thoughts are freed from the depths of the heart and the subconscious before being poured onto the page.

Literature written beyond the realms of genre he is known to grab readers; kicking, screaming, laughing or crying and drag them into his novels.

Enter the literary world of Frank Talaber.

Frank Talaber's Writing Style?

He's been known to respond with: Mix Dan Millman (Way of The Peaceful Warrior) with Charles De Lint (Moonheart) and throw in a mad scattering of Tom Robbins (Even Cowgirls Get The Blues). PS: He's better looking than Stephen King (Carrie, The Stand, It, The Shining) and his romantic stuff will have you gasping quicker than Robert James Waller (Bridges Of Madison County).

Or as is often said: You don't have to be mad to be a writer, but it sure helps.

Stillwaters Runs Deep Novel Set

Stillwaters Runs Deep Book One: Raven's Lament

Protesting the logging of an old-growth forest, an environmentalist fells a rare tree, unwittingly releasing…something…into our world. After his subsequent disappearance, reporter Brooke Grant looks for answers. During his investigation he finds the love of his life, only to lose her to, well, he doesn't really know what. Brooke enlists the aid of his love's intriguing and extraordinary shaman uncle to help save her. Only they don't only have to save her, but save the world from being changed forever.

Stillwaters Runs Deep Book Two: The Lure

Ever go out for the evening and not remember what you did? What if there was a bar where spirits can enter your inebriated body and use it until you sober up? Well such a bar exists in Stanley Park, where the city's mayor has been murdered, his family missing, a dangerous witch has been released from her centuries-old imprisonment and an intriguing and extraordinary shaman shows up, only to vanish after leaving cryptic clues. So begins Detective Carol Ainsworth's first case.

Stillwaters Runs Deep Book Three: The Awakening

How angry would a mythical god be if he found himself awakening inside a mortal? After a strange and inexplicable death inside a jail, an intriguing and extraordinary shaman detects great unrest in the world, and breaks his way into the jail to investigate. He enlists Detective Carol Ainsworth to assist as an undercover prison officer who, rather strangely, also finds herself tasked with bringing to justice the murderer of a gentle forest being's mother.

The Ainsworth Chronicles

(An urban fantasy, paranormal thriller series set in Victoria, BC.)

Ainsworth Chronicles Book One: The Joining

The Joining

Welcome to Victoria in Beautiful British Columbia, the most haunted city in North America, and to Detective Carol Ainsworth's first day undercover at the very grand old lady, The Fairmont Empress Hotel. Ready to deal with the two Italian families flying in for a wedding to unite them, she did not bargain for the ghosts, the FBI agent or the ancient curses that come along too. Add to that the very wonderful and mysterious psychic lady claiming you've invited her, the young boys disappearing, and the weird things happening to the unfortunates looking for their next fix trapped alongside spirits in the sewers, Carol found her first undercover assignment way more challenging than she could have imagined.

The one saving grace was the great Empress High Tea that Agnes introduced her to and the fabulous scones that are to die for. Literally.

Book two: The Mystery of Ms. Teak

soon to be released later 2020